I0544963

VILCORP

KRIS CHARLES

Copyright © 2020 by Katherine Rochholz
Waterloo, IA
Publisher's Note
All rights reserved as permitted under the U.S. Copyright Act of 1976. No portion of this book may be reproduced by any means, mechanical, electronic, or otherwise, without first obtaining the permission of the copyright holder.
This is a work of fiction. Any similarity to persons living or dead (unless explicitly noted) is merely coincidental.
Cover By Katherine Rochholz
ISBN: 978-1-7356249-2-1

This book is for my best friend. She has helped me more than she can ever know. Discovering the GISH and Supernatural community has helped me become myself.

This is for Tressa.

CHAPTER ONE
IN THE BEGINNING...

There was Darkness.

Then everything got muddy. Evolution. Religion. But basically, as far as cosmic timelines, in an exceptionally quick amount of time the Earth went from being a ball of rock to being able to sustain different types of life. From the first single-cell organisms to dinosaurs to humanity.

Humanity eventually ate the apple, which is just a metaphor for evolving into telling the difference between being a decent human being and being an asshole. Doubtful there was a demon disguised as a snake telling a fully developed Homo-Sapian to eat an apple. If demons, Satan, and God exist, they kept far away from humanity since the beginning.

For humanity did not just evolve into the normal beings that make up the vast majority of the world's population. In the stories of the ancestors that had been passed down, they said some humans were personally touched by God's divine grace.

That grace gave birth to the heroes and the villains.

In reality, it was a chromosomal anomaly.

But one many exploited.

Chaos reigned.

And it was glorious.

For life without chaos is like a superhero without a cause.

There used to be a time where superheros reigned over and protected the lands.

They reigned in the chaos.

They brought order.

They were loved.

For millennia.

Until the villains became corporate.

The Queen of Evil brought them together.

Brought order to chaos.

Tricked the world.

Used fear, and the fact world was evolving into industrial and corporate societies, to take power from the shadows.

For hundreds, thousands even, of years it was the typical bad guy blows something up, steals something, does something super villain-y, and the hero would come in and save the day. Very basic. Exceptionally ordinary. Citizens worshiped the heroes and hated the villains. The superheros, however, knew the chaos the villains caused gave them a cause and a reason to exist.

One villain loathed it. She hated the whole... flamboyance... of her... evilness.

Etain.

Also known as Doctor Arc.

And with that, she vowed to change the way the world work.

She was tired of the hero always winning.

She was tired of the hero lording over her.

Her arch-nemesis, who had the stupid ass name of Earth Phoenix.

It was so not her actual name.

Back then they protected their actual name. But since Phoenix was her number one enemy, she knew her actual name.

Catriona.

But she never gave it up.

After all, Catriona, was hers. She called dibs.

Then she got the villains to go corporate.

And Catriona disappeared.

But Etain kept tabs on her.

Dibs was dibs, after all.

She just never figured out she would be a villain that would need a hero.

And she for sure knew that Catriona never figured she would have the Queen of Evil asking her to save the world.

The question was, would the hero answer the villain's cry for help?

Or would this Queen Villain have to save the world on her own?

That is where the story may begin or end.

But before there was a cry for help, there was only…

THE QUEEN.

CHAPTER TWO
A QUEEN RISES

The past was just that to Etain. The past. And that is where it needed to stay. Nobody existed that knew her name, knew her origins, any longer. Either she killed them, or the warriors of her clan had killed them. So, should have found it easy enough to lie to herself she had no past.

But it was not easy.

But she still lied to herself.

The past died with the ones that made her human.

Etain had the plan to just pretend she just came into being. Nobody would really question it. People did not care where heroes and villains came from, they just praised and worshiped the heroes and feared the villains.

She thought of anything that could tie back to her existence as Etain. The journals she kept were safe with her, and always would be safe with her. All other evidence she existed burned with her village and the two surrounding it.

One thing alone remained.

She knew there was a rock carving her mother had done; they carved it into the rock near the village. It depicted two little girls, with their names carved above them. But that could never lead to her.

And she refused to destroy it, as that is where she laid her sister to rest.

The only piece of evidence. And it would be protected. Forever.

But besides that, nothing could exist of Etain.

Though Etain always knew.

She had a lot of guilt.

A lot of anger.

If she had just been there, she could have saved her sister.

Instead, she had thought of her own happiness.

She should have known better than that.

She was her father's daughter.

The good and the bad.

She should have known better than to leave her sister alone.

She should have known better than that.

She did the leaving, as was the custom in her clan, but her father made sure she felt the guilt and took the blame.

She should have known better than that.

But she bought into the fantasy.

The fantasy that she could be happy.

For that, Etain felt the need to punish herself.

She denied herself emotions.

She would get to the point she needed to feel something.

Just not numbness.

That is when she took a blade and made thin, shallow cuts upon her skin.

They would be the only evidence that she could feel.
The only evidence that she punished herself for the past.
Hidden from the world upon her covered arms and her thighs.
To the world, she had a new existence.
To start this new existence, she just went by Arc. It was a name she heard a village whisper when she passed through and shocked a man for daring to touch her.
She moved from village to village, stealing in the night. She had to survive. She had to live. She had her doubts. Doubts of how she would be known. Everything was against her.
The most powerful heroes were judge-y bastards. The villains were heartless, soulless. So what was she?
For now, she just questioned herself. She feared the people she was installing fear into would find out she was just guessing the answers she needed. Just going through motions and making it up as she went along. But for now it seemed to work. So, she continued going from village to village, being a minor villain, taking what she wanted. And for a bit of time that worked for her.
Until she knew she needed more.
She needed power.
She was so tired of not having power.
Power would protect herself.
She had always longed to have power.
She had planned on becoming the Clan Leader once upon a time.
She had watched in her village that all the power was with the Clan Leader. That they could do anything. Say anything. Act in any way they wanted. She was just lucky she had loved her loves. Her male lover was the heir to the Clan Leader. And she had him wrapped around her little finger. It would allow her to have him declare her the Clan Leader. And with that, she could have changed the laws.
But that all was destroyed in her father's greed.
Her father's want for power.
In her anger.
In her grief.
So, she had to figure a way to gain power once more.
But it was not going to be easy.
It was in her blood to want power.
She would stop at nothing to have it.
She knew she would have to tear down the obstacles in front of her, brick by brick. But she would make it. She was powerful. She was starting to be feared. And she could put on a mask that could fool the world. After all, she had a mask that fooled her Clan Leader and her father since she was a young child. She hid her powers. She protected herself. She could do it again.
But without power, she could not protect herself.
The first step was knowing exactly what her powers could do. And controlling them, even in her panic.
There were more than a few incidents where she could not get her powers to work to protect her in her panic. Men were barbarians. Taking what they want with no care. Not that women were much better. She did not want to live this way. She did not want to just exist. She did not want to be nameless. She had powers that could move mountains

if she wanted. She had powers that could kill the Earth. So, why was she not grabbing the power owed to her?

She needed to control her powers, to have power.

She needed power.

So, why was she just standing there?

Why was she just surviving?

Was she afraid of what it would cost to cross that last line?

Had she not already crossed that last line?

She longed for powers.

She was going to change the way of life for her people.

That dream was dead.

But why was she still standing at the shallow end of life?

She made her choice.

She would no longer hold back.

And nobody would ever make her feel powerless again.

Never.

So, she started to attack small villages; she killed the rapists and abusers.

She fought the monsters, the ones who took with no care, no mercy, but in the process she would become the monster.

She sat at the base of a bare tree in a cemetery. Nobody walked the cemetery after dark; this allowed her to watch the villages. Burying the bodies was a new thing, before most just burned them. But she did like the idea of burying them. They had buried her sister. Not just burned like garbage. She sat waiting for her clothes to dry. She did not care she was naked under the moonlight. She sat there in the dark, her eyes glowing and her hair blowing behind her. She watched the village that was her first target. People would rue the day they hurt her.

They would rue the day she lost what grounded her to humanity.

They would no longer witness her good and bad.

A tear fell down her cheek as she knew that after tonight, her hopes and dreams were forever gone.

She would carry the guilt.

The hurt.

And it would fuel her rise to the top.

For now, humanity would only witness her at her worst.

They would only witness her in POWER.

She sat wondering about many things. She was told the gods and Norns controlled their lives. She was told three women held the threads of life. It was not a new concept. She had to wonder about the Norns. Why they put in the pain and heartache into her thread.

She heard the voice in her mind that sounded like her sister saying she did not need to go this path.

But the other voice, the darker one, was louder, telling her she needed power to never be hurt again. And her soul's grief, the ripped apart pieces of what was left of her soul uses as threads to hold together this black heart of hers, was enough to drown out that light in her soul. The light that was there because of the love she felt for three people in her life. All three gone and that thread that tethered her to the light cut. She vowed to no longer be the Norn's bitch. They would never cut her thread. She was given life by the Earth goddess, and until the Earth goddess chose to no longer connect to her soul and took her power away, she would live and fight.

And gain the power needed to protect herself.

Come dawn, she attacked the first village.

She came in looking like an angel bathed in light.

A Hero.

She smirked as they soon learned otherwise.

She showed her power. She made all fear her, fear that she would come to their village, destroy, kill, steal, and leave devastation in her wake. She seemed to kill at random. But she had watched the village for weeks before attacking each time. She fought. She took on their warriors and won. Those battles did destroy locations, but if people watched, they would have noticed she did not destroy housing. She did not destroy their crops. She went to destroy those who abused their powers to hurt. But that did not make her a hero. She did not want to give them redemption. She killed them. She was not a hero. She did not believe in second chances. She killed. She would release all those from a fate similar to her sister. So, she killed.

And since she wanted to survive, she stole. She took what she needed and wanted. So, she fought and battled. She licked her wounds. But this allowed her to be feared. It allowed her to test her powers.

She could be injured and had been many times, but she always healed. Always. The powers granted to her by the Earth Goddess healed her.

But then she found a much simpler way when she was but eighteen.

Sex.

Give a man or woman sex, and they practically gave her what she wanted. She first tried this with a clan leader and when he passed out after she dominated him and gave him his orgasm; she took what she wanted.

The reason she had tried it out was she had been at the community grouping drinking their ale and he had come up and was obvious in his desire to have her. She knew if they had been alone and not amongst others drinking, he would have tried to rape her. As it was, he was aggressive. She knew what she wanted was in his housing. So, why not try to get there by allowing him sex? She drank until she was numb. Then she let him take her back to his housing. Where she used the ropes to tie him up as she took him in her body. It was not unpleasant. She rode him hard, trying to get him to finish as soon as possible, and even felt mild enjoyment herself. When they had finished, he passed out, and she left town with her prize.

It began a serious of one-night stands. A series of 'relationships' where she benefited. She gained power. She gained wealth. She even gained a few titles in her life, becoming politically powerful, and even for a brief stint controlling the leaders, royalty, whoever was in power.

All using sex.

She had been able to wrap some of the world's most powerful men and women around her fingers. She hardly had to attack villages anymore. Her Queen of Evil title had been easy to obtain once she used sex to gain a better position in life.

But she was still a villain. She would cover her face and ravage the lands, killing those who were far from innocent and taking what was of value. She even used those men and women of power wrapped around her fingers, and they too raged wars for her. It was fantastic.

It was empowering.

It protected her from the evils of humanity.

It was not long before the name Arc was feared. It was not long before she could walk down a street and be respected as if she were a Queen. And as she closed her emotions off more and more, as she allowed herself to become numb. Using liquors, drugs, sex, she gained more and more power. All to make sure she never had to have her heart ripped out like it was all those years ago.

But at night she could not lie to herself. The nightmares of what her sister must have gone through, of what she had gone through when she had run. So many centuries, millennium, and in the harsh light of her mind, her past was never really over. She just traveled the world, as more and more land was discovered. She had the powers to do so with no coin from her purse.

She was a mess.

But she did her best to lie to herself that she was more than fine, and she was the one in power.

Not her past.

Not her father.

Not her emotions.

But her mind.

She was in power.

She was; no matter what truths screamed in her ears during her nightmares.

She lost her self-control at times running from her past. She knew she had to draw lines in the sand. At least one line. A line she would not cross.

She was a mess.

She was not a fool.

The past was the past.

And she would not let it have control of her again.

She would stop losing her self-control.

She would make sure she did not ever cross her own self-imposed line.

She may not have many morals.

But she did have some.

Never hurt an innocent.

Never hurt a kid.

All those that lost their lives deserve what she would do to them.

It was time for the Queen to rise.

It was time to be her strongest in the moments she felt like falling to her grief.

To be strong in the face of her pain.

To be her strongest when she wants to be weak.

The Queen had to rise.

And the Queen rose.

Pushing the past into the back of her mind.
Hiding her emotions behind liquor, drugs, and sex.
Etain no longer existed but as a memory.
Long live Doctor Arc, Queen of Evil.
Long Live The Queen...

CHAPTER THREE
THE FIRST MEETING

Catriona smiled, she was finally eighteen. She had been training for this moment. She was now fully into her powers, and her village had given her the name Earth Phoenix. She had just gotten word there was a disturbance in the next village over. The Queen of Evil Doctor Arc was causing trouble.

Doctor Arc was one of the oldest of villains.

She was also undefeated.

But Catriona still was naïve. So, she used her powers and took to the sky; it was time to show the villain there was a new hero in this world. And this hero would not stand for Arc's bullshit.

Etain was having fun. She had been bored, and this tiny village claimed to be protected by a new hero. She wanted to meet this hero. So, she planned an attack. She just walked into the village and started shooting electrical currents in the air. Not hurting anybody, just destroying. How the world missed she never actually killed anybody who was innocent she did not know. But it did give her a nice reputation, one she used to become feared by heroes and villains alike.

And then she heard the new hero come. She flipped around and held a bolt of electricity in her hand. They took away her breath. This new hero was gorgeous. This hero had a warm sepia skin tone, the undertones were an orange red. Her eyes were a honey burgundy brown. Etain wanted nothing more than to see her blush. Perhaps she could turn this little hero. But she needed time to plot, so she just smiled and winked. "You are mine, for eternity." Etain then disappeared from view and left the tiny village to plot the next encounter.

Catriona was confused, she turned up, and the villain stated one line and left. She turned to help the citizen put out fires and put things into order. She was confused. Why would the villain who was feared even amongst the oldest of heroes just leave when she showed up? Catriona had heard stories of Arc, but had not been prepared to see the beauty before her.

Arc's blue eyes were a white blue, like ice, or the electrical currents she controlled. Her hair was like a dark flame, and her skin that was fair, so fair one could see the cool silverish blue veins upon what parts of her chest that were exposed, with the most captivating rose painting her cheeks. Then just to say, 'you are mine, for eternity,' and then leave. Catriona tried to push it out of her mind, but she felt that something major just happened, something that would change the course of her life forever.

Etain entered her lair and sat down on her throne. She knew her minions would not ask questions. She had created an illusion and spent some time asking about the new hero. Found out her name was Earth Phoenix. And better yet, she found the village she came from. Which meant she could send her minions to get her proper name.

She had never had that reaction to a hero, or anybody since her first loves. She looked at her minions. "Spread word, the new hero, Earth Phoenix, is mine! Any villain, hero, or mortal that touches her will find my wrath."

"Yes, Queen!" They yelled before rushing off and spreading the world.

Etain went to her office and sat down. Her minions never got to be in her house. She pulled out her journal and created an entry, as she had every day since she was taught to write under the cover of darkness by her mother.

'The nightmares still plague me. What is one more nightmare in this three thousand year long life? Thankfully, I do not have to have much sleep, for when I do, all I see is the event that created this evil. And I wake up sweating more than a demon in a confessional. Sometimes I wonder if it is my nightmares the fuel me. Other times I know it is my anger and hatred towards a man I killed almost three thousand years ago. Nothing changes in this life. That is… until today.

Today I met a new hero. And the punch in the gut I received was like nothing I had felt before. It was like I had electrocuted myself. I had not felt that since the first time I laid eyes upon Bridgid and Drest when I was eight, and knew I would marry them.

This new hero would make a good conquest, but something held me back from fighting her today. Perhaps I will another day. But something tells me, I will let this hero win, just so can keep seeing her again and again.

Instead, I teeter on the edge of whatever type of madness she has sparked inside my soul. The smallest thing will push me into releasing whatever comes from that madness. Either the sheer vileness that I know surrounds the light of my soul, or the honest truth of emotions shall erupt from my soul like a volcano.

Perhaps tomorrow I will unleash my darkness.

Unleash my powers at full strength.

The question is, will tomorrow ever come?

For all I want is to see her.

I must be careful.

For the taste of love…

Love?

No.

This is lust.

But the taste of love is bittersweet.

And it is no different with lust.

When all I see is the darkness of my soul, something comes back to remind me I am but a human, gifted or not, and I am not exempt from feeling human emotions of lust. It is time to go have another fling. Perhaps that will get this hero off my mind.'

Etain looked at the ancient language, one that has all but died out. It predated the Celtic languages of Ireland. She had been born in the Early Bronze Age after all, and the Celts came near the end. Nobody from that time was around anymore. The practically immortal e and villains had been killed, and she remained. Mostly because she killed them. Any connection to her life before she let her powers known by killing those who broke her, heart, mind, and soul, had to be destroyed.

Etain shivered once more, thinking of her past. It was cold out. She always did hate the cold. But she stayed in chilly places. Mostly because the ice and snow could buffer her powers if she lost control of them during her night terrors. She did not have many anymore, but enough that she did not want to take any chances.

Etain hated the cold. The chill in the air had nothing really to do with the child in her soul when she thought of the past. She could not get warm at this time, this chill it went bone deep.

She was sure it was just grief she has refused to deal with even after three thousand years, and being reminded of her past loves brought terrible memories to the surface.

She hated the cold.

Heat was easy to deal with; she could strip off her clothes and lay in the sun, maybe even by a lake, and get a tan. She could lay naked in the sun, or moon, and let the winds cool the sweat upon her body. Or she could strip and dive into the pool, or the lake, or an ocean even.

When she dives deep into the cool water, she would come back to the surface feeling refreshed. Like the glacial water washed away, just for the moment, all the weight on her shoulders. For a moment, the cold in her soul was helping to cool her down, to remind her she was human, and she was alive.

But the cold...

She shivered as she wrapped her arms around herself; the cold was hell.

For the cold, there was nothing she could do to escape that. It clutched at her like death's claws and laughed at her as her lips turned blue. She had been in a few places, where no matter the layers, no matter the body heat, and no matter the temperature, the cold went deep into her bones as if preparing her for death.

Each time she fought the cold of death.

But the cold filling her bones tonight was a different type.

It was not the fear of death.

No, she knew that cold all too well in the spots she had been in during her time traveling this world full of imperfect beings.

No, this cold was a deep soul cutting grief that comes with losing the only people that kept her grounded. Kept her moral. Kept her from building her powers up enough to be so feared that people called her Queen. And that cold...

She didn't know exactly how to fight.

So, she just waited for the memories to pass. The nightmare to come. Then she would take it and shove it all back into the darkest parts of her mind, stick that part of her back into the cage in the darkness of her mind, and ignore it until it reminded her once more of the darkest day of her life.

She stood up. She had to do something. She left the lair with an outfit for the time, of course, a noble woman, used to money and riches. She did enjoy the finer things of life. It did not take her long to end up in a village that had a celebration going on. She found a woman with darker skin and, after drinking herself to the point of numbness, took her to her bed.

Had she ever been sober when she had sex since she was eighteen?

She could not remember, even with an eidetic memory like hers, three thousand years of memories get jumbled and lost in her mind. It was another reason she always wrote in her journals.

She pushed the thoughts away. She had a substitute for the one she wanted in her bed, naked in said bed. She smirked at the woman. Tonight would be good for some stress relief.

Evil did not change after all.

Evil was evil.

She knew the one she wanted in the bed would never be there.

Not unless she did the impossible and got a pure soul to fall.

For tonight, this woman with darkened skin was enough to sate her restlessness.

The next morning, Etain left the woman and was back at her lair. She thought sex would have pushed the thoughts of that new hero from her mind. Alas, thoughts of that new little goody two shoes were still floating in her head. Sex had always worked before. What was it about this hero?

Something had to be done about these thoughts in her head.

Time for another attack.

Etain enjoyed watching Phoenix as she kept throwing punches at her. Sometimes Etain let them hit. But she was just playing. She watched her fighting style. Phoenix would have to be protected for a long while. Phoenix was still young and thus needed time to perfect her fighting style. Etain made a note to send some martial artists she knew from Asia to train Phoenix. She would have to wipe their minds exactly who hired them, but it was worth the risk. After all, Etain could not risk another stupid ass villain or hero messing with her Earth Phoenix.

She had called dibs.

And Etain knew villains liked to push boundaries. She was a villain, and she never listened to the others dibs. She battled heroes as they messed with her plans. She did not seek them out, but she never let them win. She expected some issues with a few villains. Nothing that Etain could not handle, but it would be annoying.

She would go to Asia tomorrow.

Let the sweet little hero think she gained their eye with her potential. Which may be true if they heard of her fighting in a few months, but Etain was not a patient person. Never had been, never truly will be.

There was a martial artist that was known to make deals.

He was a powered martial artist. He was not a hero, but he was not a villain either. But a deal with the devil to make sure Phoenix could protect herself was better than not making a deal at all and taking the risk of losing Phoenix.

Etain got a good hit in on Phoenix, and it threw her into a wall of rock. "Get up, little hero!"

Phoenix was gasping for breath. She did not know if she could get up. Arc was just too powerful. She did not know if she could make it out alive. She thought about leaving, to fight another day.

"You do not get to think about leaving, little hero. You have a choice. You can either roll over and die. I can make your death quick. Or you can keep fighting. No matter what, you keep fighting. So, get up, little hero. Or you are not a hero but a fraud."

That pissed Phoenix off. She pushed herself up and threw herself back into battle.

Etain laughed and let it go for a while. She smirked as they both stood upon the ground. "Good job, little hero." She got close and laughed, "your are mine, for eternity." With that, Etain disappeared once more.

Etain felt more alive during the battle than she had since she became Arc. But, honestly, this hero was getting her wrapped around her little finger. She had to leave. She had an ego on her, but honestly, no self-respecting villain let a hero win like she let Phoenix win today. Oh, Etain was no fool. She knew she would make the same terrible choice and start a battle to just see the pretty new hero. And then let the hero think she won. She just had to be more prepared next time for the emotions, so the dear Phoenix did not catch on to what was happening.

A villain falling for a hero?

It could not happen.

For Etain had her moments of happiness over three thousand years ago.

But she knew she would fall to the temptation of seeing the pretty hero again.

However, today's plans were to move to a new location for a while, drink coffee, and try not to stab any of the minions for asking stupid questions. Like asking the new hero out as her persona. Stupid minion. Do they not know that a light as bright as a Phoenix should not be dragged into the dark? Once a hero sees true darkness, takes that one step into the darkness, they are never the same again. And Etain did not want to be responsible for that step in Phoenix's growth.

For a complete bitch, she could be decent.

However, Phoenix would be protected.

After all, she called dibs.

Though at times, Etain wondered who would ever save her?

Was she worth saving?

Then the reality of her existence would smack her in the face. She did not have to be saved. She did not have to submit. She would never submit. She was not a damsel in distress. She could slay her own goddamn demons.

She would never allow herself to fall to that weakness again.

Never.

CHAPTER FOUR
A THOUGHT IS BORN

Etain was bored with the life she had lived for almost three thousand years. She became a villain in one moment. It was not something subtle. It was not her trying to do what was best for the greater good, and she found herself the villain. She had been happy with her boring life. She had hidden her powers from her power hungry father. She had been born at a time since that would become known as the Early Bronze Age. However, her family was landowners and farmers. Her father loved lording over people. Life was basic. She had been happy. She had her little sister; she had a young woman in the village she had been in love with, a male friend who was going to marry them both so they could all live together, and most of all she had her happiness.

It was common to have multiple wives.

What was not common was that the three of them actually loved each other.

She had been lucky.

Until that day.

Until her life came crashing down.

Of course it did. After all, she could not have happiness. So, she vowed nobody would be able to rip her heart out again like they had been able to with her sister, with her girlfriend, with her future husband. She vowed to close herself off.

Instead, she fought.

She destroyed.

She became the villain of her story.

But she was still determined to win.

Heroes fought her. Battled her. Tried to destroy her. That was a hero's job in the end when everything is said and done to defeat the villain. Some say there comes a day where even the strongest and most powerful will die. That they should stop the wars, the battles. It was not about avoiding battle; it was not about avoiding war; it was about winning. Pure and simple, everything in life is about winning. One is either the winner or the loser. There is no second place in life. No participation points. There is a winner. A loser. The one who lives or the one who dies. And she would let nobody take her life.

She would let nobody have that power over her soul. She remembered the stories passed down. That killing someone gave you their soul. Their power. Their life force. She always believed it was bullshit. But she would not take the risk that someone could have her soul, her power, her life, and most of all, her power.

So, she killed many humans. Villains. Heroes. Killing them was a choice in self perseveration. After all, letting them live to fight another day meant another chance for them to gain her life and soul from her. She had made a name for herself amongst the villains. They respected her. She became a leader, a voice among them, even if they all worked separately from each other.

And she reveled in the power.

After all, she was the Queen of Evil.

A title given to her by the normal people. The ones who feared all those with talents. Though they worshiped the heroes, they did so out of fear. Not respect. And though she was feared, not a single person dare to disrespect her when she showed up in their little corner of the world.

Queen of Evil.

She reveled in that title. People feared her. She had destroyed anybody who knew her true identity. Nobody knew her.

Everybody knew her as Arc. And later on, Doctor Arc, mostly due to the fact that at some point in time the ordinary people started giving all villains and heroes whatever name they wanted. And most went with it. Just easier to keep their names safe.

Though there were few villains that were as known as she was in this world. And those were the ones she was trying to get a chance to talk to. But villains are not known for playing nice with each other. Basically, long enough to get an orgasm. Same in neutral territories with heroes. Sex was a pastime of heroes and villains alike.

The blood pumping, knowing it was going to end in a draw?

Fly off and have a good time.

Have an orgasm.

Leave to fight another day.

Neutral was a joke word. Most of the time those heroes became corrupted and became villains. Or were killed.

Heroes… they were human, too. And everybody had a price.

Everybody.

Some just had a higher cost that others is all.

Etain worked hard to become the most feared villain in this world. And villains and heroes alike feared her. She could kill with a blink. She could fly. She was a deadly woman who had no emotions to hold her back from gaining the ultimate control. Her father had taught her one thing. Making others fear her was the only way to get ahead in life. The only way to prevent self-destruction was to shut off emotions. Shutting down emotions was just one step into becoming feared. Becoming feared lead to having almost unlimited power.

And power was what she craved.

But her existence had become boring. Routine. Affairs to gain power, money, whatever she needed at the time. Battles with both sides. Choosing Minions to go on suicide missions. Blowing up towns, cities, villages, all in the name of being bored. She understood why some beings that were basically immortal killed themselves. Life as an immortal was boring. Even as she watched the world change decade by decade, century by century, millennia by millennia. There were so many changes that she could not deny, but those new shiny people and advancements could only hold her attention long enough for her to say, 'oh, shiny!'

It all changed when she first came across an eighteen-year-old hero named Earth Phoenix. She was a brand new shiny hero. It revealed a bit of her powers during each battle. At first, she seemed to be a very annoying hero, like all the others. But, Etain had to admit, this one was cute. So, she called dibs. And had to know everything about

her. Everything. Including her proper name and identity. Each little
battle, each piece of news on this Earth Phoenix revealed a bit about
who she was, and it led Etain to her village.

So, she had a plan to send her minions into the town to find her
name.

But she had to get that precious little hero out of the village.

So, she attacked.

The village next to her target's village was at the base of a
volcano. Etain decided that Doctor Arc needed to send a message.

And what a battle.

The punches thrown.

The jibs.

The flirting.

The villain known as Doctor Arc smirked at the superhero known as
Earth Phoenix. Oh, Etain knew she was in lust with this hero, that she
stopped denying at least. She also knew that this hero considered her
the Queen of Evil, well most heroes concurred with that statement. She
loved the name and allowed the stories and rumors to spread.

Doctor Arc finally had an arch rival. Perhaps some day when she
succeeds in her plan to take over the world, she will keep this
superhero as her pet. Okay, so she would keep her safe. She wanted
only willing people in her bed. She became a villain because of
someone raping and killing her sister. She would never force someone
to be in her bed.

Never.

She had some morals. Not a lot and she could offer nobody moral
support because of the lack of morals, but she did have some morals.
She had rules of life. Do not hurt kids. Do not rape. Do not allow men
to make women sub-servant. And never trust anybody but herself, so she
could never get hurt again. She knew deep down it was all fear, fear
of losing people she cared for once more. But what she feared even
more, was that she would care more for them more than they would care
for her. Then her world turned upside down.

Since this beauty known as Earth Phoenix came of age with her
powers, she had been a thorn in Etain's side. She would always end up
going up against her. And something within Etain's conscience would
not let her actually kill the new hero.

Etain would admit, however, life was finally a bit more
interesting. One could only have so many one-night stands with
villains and heroes alike. She would never degrade herself to sleep
with a normal mortal.

"What has you smirking, Arc?" Catriona sneered. They were in a
middle of a battle. And Doctor Arc just floated there, relaxed as
could be, and had a smirk on her face.

Why were they battling? Arc had sent an electric surge through
the ground to set off a volcano. Catriona had capped it and contained
it, barely. If she hadn't had the ability over matter, then the town
would have been lost.

"I got you where I want you, Pheonix." And Etain had this beauty
where she wanted her. Away from her village and distracted.

"And how do you figure that, Arc?" Catriona spat out as she tried
to contain any shock-waves. There were going to be quite a few, due to

the fact that Capitan Arc had used the electric currents from the core to cause a series of earthquakes to set off the volcano.

"You are being distracted by me, while my minions get my what I sent them after," Etain laughed as she brought herself to the ground. Etain knew her flying was just a pallor trick with the electric currents within the Earth's atmosphere. Phoenix did not know that it was a trick. In fact, Phoenix was not one hundred percent sure what her powers were, and Etain was still figuring out what all Phoenix had in her arsenal. That was the toughest thing when dealing with a newly borne hero. Figuring out what their powers were and how to defeat them. At least Earth Phoenix was some nice eye candy.

"What are they doing, Arc?" Catriona was just exhausted. Sometimes dealing with Arc was too much to handle. Arc messed with her mind and emotions. The flirting was the worst part, especially since Catriona knew that Arc was her type; if she was not the Queen of the Villains.

"Getting me one tiny piece of information. Nothing too evil, Phoenix, baby."

Catriona growled, "stop flirting and tell me!"

"Nothing to concern you. Only the minions shall die. None of your precious humans." After all, the piece of information she wanted none of her minions could live, only she should know this information. The piece of information was concerning her precious Earth Phoenix. Honestly, most villains thought minions were disposable, and Etain was no different in this thought. Etain hired a lot of brawn, but some smarts. This time around, she sent a few of her smartest minions with a bunch of brawn. They were to get her Phoenix's name and then, well, their deaths would be quick… ish.

Catriona growled and went to throw another attack when Etain disappeared. She sighed and dropped the attack; she turned to help the citizens of the devastated town. Catriona helped clean up the village, helped contain the aftershocks of the devastation from Doctor Arc. How could someone turn out that evil?

Etain saw the signal that her minions were successful and she used another pallor trick to appear to disappear, causing the electrical currents around her to create a shield that made her invisible. That had taken her a thousand years to learn how to do. However, it was only after Phoenix that she let the world see the trick.

She now had her minions in front of her. She smirked as they told her the name of her Phoenix. Catriona O'Consaidín. Last names. They really started around a couple hundred years ago. She really did not understand the use. Etain had been born when she had been called the daughter of her father, and would have become known as the first wife of her husband.

"Madam? What will you have us do now that you have Earth Phoenix's identity? Kill her?"

That caused a fury to flow through Etain. "How could you suggest such a thing? She is the only entertainment and excitement I have in this world." She caused a charge to go through the ground and stop the hearts of all her minions. She was glad she had been planning to leave this lair and set up a new base. She was not even going to deal with the bodies. She wondered what people would say in another thousand years when they found the cave.

She swept out and went to her house. Perhaps it was time to leave home. She had stayed on this island for a long time.

She turned when Prince John, Lord of Ireland, came in with a smirk on his face. She knew what that meant. This man had a power as well, but it was of being able to control those who were not powered with his voice. She had taken him as a lover, but she was tired of him. It was time to end this sexual relationship and move onto the next phase of her life.

She moved her documents into a locked drawer. They were plans of a thought of organizing the villains, creating a company and ruling class within those who have powers.

A thought had been born as she watched the British Empire grow. "John, I was thinking, though this affair is beneficial to me, it is time for you to prepare to take the throne. After all, why should your siblings keep the throne? There are many who wish revenge. Give one of them a crossbow with an arrow dipped in Belladonna. He will die, and as he has no legitimate children, you shall become King. It is time to lose the name John Lackland and become King John. With a new wife. Have an annulment due to consanguinity, seize her property, and then marry the granddaughter of Louis VI. Have her give birth to your heirs. Then your legacy will end with you being a King. Not just the favored son of a King who had his throne stolen from him from his rebellious, traitorous brother."

John looked at his mistress. "Will it work?"

"Of course it will. Not only do you have a silver tongue ability, but you have the power to be king. Lord of Ireland to become King of England."

John kissed her hard. "I guess this is our last night together, my dear?"

"It is for the best." She pulled him down for a kiss, her thoughts all on her plans, and how she would leave the bed with all the jewels, gold, and silver this man had given her over the last three years.

She left the bed in the dead of night. It was the Devil's Hour, but she was not afraid. She had already figured out her soul was damned to whatever hellish punishment awaited the wicked. She was also sure she would not, if she ever met one, make a deal with a demon. Maybe become its lover; just so when she did go to her hellish punishment, she would have a connection in her bid to gain power after death. Thankfully, however, she was practically immortal, so the thought of Dubnos did not cause her any doubts. She knew the moment she destroyed the villages at just thirteen that she would never see Albios. So, she focused on controlling Bitu.

She looked down at the last thing she grabbed before going out to her horse, a stack of parchment. On the very first page there was one word: VilCorp.

CHAPTER FIVE
EVIL GOES CORPORATE

Etain may have been Celtic, well, pre-Celtic, but close enough if one wanted to label the beliefs she grew up with as a child. But she had to admit Latin combined better with an evolving language. VilCorp was born from the idea of the word corporatus, which is to form a body. She was working on getting villains to listen to her about setting up an alliance of sorts, not that anybody would trust each other, and she would have a controlling interest in this alliance. However, the issue she was running into was most villains had issues with trusting the Queen of Evil.

She did not blame them; she had killed many heroes and villains. She was not known for compassion or fairness. She had to figure out a way for them to listen to her. More than just fear. Though fear is good. Best way? VilCorp on a smaller level. She smirked as she started buying up land. If offering goods, gold, whatever their little hearts desired, did not work, she took it over by seizing it through fear and destruction. Though sometimes she let that cute little hero going around as Earth Phoenix win.

Just so they could battle on another day.

Etain looked up at the sky. She had been trying to get all the villains that were the most powerful together. She got fourteen to come. There was a blood red ring around the moon. She always remembered what her mother stated about a ring around the moon. When there was a ring around the moon, something wicked was coming their way. Etain smirked. She was that something wicked. She really did not have a choice in that matter anymore. She had been the villain for too long. Had done some of the worst things in the world. She had done even things she regretted.

The question was, would the other villains listen.

For the first meeting, the answer was an obvious NO.

It broke out into a bloody free-for-all battle.

Which got the attentions of the heroes.

Which just caused fifteen minor battles to start up.

There was only one positive aspect about when the villain's hero showed up. They stopped fighting with each other.

Etain signed as she just grabbed Phoenix and disappeared about a hundred miles away. Using the electrical currents in the air to hit the stream of air that blew them away from the battles quickly. She let Phoenix go. "Another time, Dove." And she disappeared again.

Catriona did not understand Arc. She would pick a battle and then, when it was getting to the point of actually hurting each other, she left. It was like she was trying to train Phoenix. Like she was protecting her. Catriona thought about going back to the battles, but there were fourteen other heroes there. So Catriona went home. Her mind a mess as she thought about Arc.

Etain sat in her lair, furious. More than one minion had been shocked for asking stupid questions. She sat upon her throne and looked out at her minions. Her fingers were tapping upon the arm of the throne. She sighed. How could she get these dumb ass villains to listen to her? She knew she had to unite the majority of the major villains. It was the only way VilCorp, and the taking over of the world, would work. She stood up and swept from the lair. She was going to go out and find out some blackmail on those fucking idiots that she, unfortunately, depended on to make VilCorp a reality.

Etain sat down and sipped her coffee. It was strong and dark and perfect. It was so strong for a solid five minutes she had hope that life would get better. Then one of her minions walked into the lair and told her that some villain wanted to have a talk with her. "Which one?"

"The one that dresses up as as that posh overlord with a face mask. Like he is trying to make it a fashion." The minion answered as he handed her another cup of coffee.

"Stuck up asshole. He calls himself Overlord. Send him in." Etain waved her hand and then whistled for her wolves to come in. They took their place by her sides.

Overlord walked in and bowed his head to Etain. "Doctor Arc."

"What do you want, Richard?" It was a subtle power trip. She knew his name, they did not know her name.

"Your plan to have us allied together. Are you still trying to make that a reality?"

"Why, Richard?" Etain sat back and crossed her legs, the slit in her dress showing her long legs. Insanely brazen for the times they were in now, but totally tame compared to other times she had lived in.

Richard found his eyes running over her legs before being started back to reality by her clearing her throat. "I want in on it. I think you are right. It would give us power, money, jewels, and whatever we want. The heroes keep winning our battles, we keep licking our wounds. Even the new one has you on the run."

Etain sat up and let her power run over her body. "I am playing with the new hero. I could kill her in a heartbeat. But I do like to play with my food. I am not the most sane. Want to suck up to me a little better, Richard?"

"Who says I am sucking up, Arc?"

"You came and bowed to me. You fear me. You want to be one of the top in the alliance. So, tell me Richard, are you sucking up?"

Richard cursed to himself. "Yes. Fine. I want in on the ground floor."

Etain smirked and moved and switched which leg was crossed. She knew she was walking sex. She made sure people thought of sex when they looked at her. Not that she would ever sleep with anybody she was planning on a working relationship with in the future. She cocked her head and thought for a moment. "What do you bring to the table? I mean, I was getting you fourteen together because I want to see who would become the power with me."

"I bring almost ten thousand minions, and property. We would be able to build more of those… companies?" At Etain's nod, he continued. "on the properties."

"You would give the property to VilCorp? Make it collective? Give up your sole claim on the land?"

"For power, a bit of a sacrifice of land now, will pay me back tenfold down the road." Richard knew that what he was saying was fact.

Etain nodded. That much was true. "Fine. But we have to convince the other thirteen. After all, a supreme council of fifteen will make sure that we never have a tie that I, as majority owner, have to break. I will be the deciding vote each time, make no mistake about that. But we do want to be fair. We are going to rule the world after all." Etain smirked, she stood and walked over to Richard. "Now to get the rest on board." She smirked and then walked out of the lair.

Etain felt a spark of life in her dead soul. Her plans were coming to fruit! The spark was bringing back that flame of interest in life again! Between the new hero that sent sparks through her soul, and now Richard, one of the richest of the Villains agreeing to bow to her! Perhaps this flame would stay this time.

But she had a feeling she just could not shake. Though this new phase of her life was just about to start, it would not last. She could not wait for this new phase. But at the same time she dreaded it.

She stopped in front of her mirror. What would life be like if she had not let the dark drown the light of her life? What if she had let the light in? Would she have gotten to know this new hero?

She shook her head. 'Stop going down that road, Etain. You made your choice. You choose this. And your Karma is that your emotions are closed off for good.'

"Your highness?" Her current lover walked out of the bathroom.

"Honey," Etain looked at the woman. She had no fucking clue what her name was any longer. "Let's go out and get something to eat and drink. We will come back here, make a little love…"

"Oh! Yes!" The woman came up and kissed her before going to get dressed.

Etain watched her go. She had to go. After tonight, Etain would pay off her father to marry her off to some rich guy. The poor woman would have affairs with her servants for life. But hey, that was life.

And life actually changed rather humanity wanted it to or not.

Life found a way to either save a person or damn a person.

The sad part was, with the times people were living in, those not the same were all damned to live a life of lies.

Unless one happened to be a hero or villain.

They could do whatever, whenever, they wanted.

But for now, Etain had her first villain under her thumb, and hopefully soon the rest would follow along.

It took another five hundred years to get the villains all seated here. In this time, Etain had bought up most of the land around the countries, not just cities. She wore the height of seventeenth century fashion. It was the seventeenth century in this new turn of life, and Etain had seen when the clock had reset to zero. She smirked as she sat down and greeted the villains.

"Welcome, once more." She looked out at the fourteen other villains that answered the call. A new villain who had killed the previous one, James, was quite excited sitting to her left. Richard to her right.

"What are we doing here, Doctor Arc?" Paul asked, as he drank the wine in front of him.

"We are here to discuss the future, VilCrop. I have been buying up land, up boats, up everything that could possibly make money and give power. You all will have a chance to have a two percent share in the company. Two percent will equal a lot of power and money."

"So, let me get this straight, fourteen of us at two percent is twenty-eight percent. And you get seventy-two percent?" Athena asked, as she sat back and folded her arms.

"No. It is two percent spread across you, twelve. As you are coming late to the party, Richard has been by my side for five hundred years. So, that is twenty-four percent. Richard gets ten percent. James, who joined about fifty years ago, gets five percent. That equals, thirty-nine percent to my sixty-one. It is my land. My money. My power that is creating this company. And you all will get a say, a voice, and power. Lots, and lots of power."

"Why should it not be equal?"

"Are you going to give all your gold, all your money, all your property for this? I have. And I will continue to do so. I mean, I have my tastes, but as you know, I am feared by all. So, today, I give you your last chance. Join us. Or…" Etain shrugged, then smirked. "Face the consequences." Etain looked at them, and could practically smell their fear. Etain did so love her reputation. Even if nobody knew the fact that no matter how wrong the reputation was, she did not kill without reason.

It took three hours for all of them to sign.

The names glistened upon the contract; she made them sign in blood. She had learned from her mother, grandmother, and great-grandmother there is magic in using blood. She believed that. She did not believe in much, but she did believe in that.

For blood carried pieces of the soul, pieces of power, without blood the being would die, their soul destroyed, their powers drained.

There was a reason that Countess Elizabeth Bathory de Esced, felt that drinking and bathing in the blood of former virgins she killed was the ticket to eternal youth. Former virgins, Etain knew Bathory's tastes, for Bathory had tried to have Etain picked up by her guards. Etain went and visited the woman and told her exactly who was off limits to her craziness: Etain, who was going by Lady Jonet Verch Leuan, and Earth Pheonix.

Etain looked down upon the glistening names, knowing they all just gave up another little piece of their soul to the darkness of creation.

Richard Harrison
James Wilson
Jerome Holmes
Harrita Albertson
Robert Evanson
Edward Nash
Kenya Ababio
Zane Gbeho
Aki Han
Chan Ming Zhang

Juan Martínez de Palategui
Diego López de Olivares
Howard Yang
Juan de Palencia
Fourteen names that just signed their soul away. Etain finally got the start of VilCorp. Not just an idea. But the true start. They controlled Europe, Asia, and Africa. But there is a new world now discovered. And soon they will rule that too.

Though first, they had to build their company.

And stop the melodrama of starting battles that the heroes always seemed to win. No matter how many times they should have lost.

And they did.

The battles stopped.

The silver-tongues started.

And soon they had the ears of the world power.

They had the money.

They could get away with anything.

And Etain started turning a blind eye.

So much so, that she ran off to the Colonies when Earth Phoenix did, claiming to set up land and companies there.

She let the fires of power burn.

She had counted the minutes, the hours, the days, to make this plan of hers into a reality. And she had a feeling one day she would watch it all go up in flames.

And she would just watch it and let it all burn.

She would light the fire.

But for now, she enjoyed the power.

She let the fires of power burn.

Etain did not know it then, but it would come back and bite her in the ass.

She was so focused on running from home, that she lost herself. And lost why she started doing what she had been doing to be cast as the villain. She locked more of her soul away. And focused on VilCorp.

And time marched on.

One thousand years. It took one thousand years to get to this point. The first five hundred were getting them to listen. The next five hundred were creating and growing her company. And hiding the fact there were villains and heroes in this world.

She destroyed proof they existed.

They were just myths.

Myths that would become the stories of entertainment.

She had lit the fire under the other villains and they had won. In the end, they had won.

For all the hero grandstanding, for all the lost battles, the villains, it appeared, had won the war.

But even as Etain ran, she knew it was going to come crashing down.

This temporary win.

For there was only so long one could hide their wicked ways.

Hide their evil from the world.

One day the world would wake up.

Or a hero would.

Her only hope was that she would still be alive at the end of the war.

But for now she cruised through the centuries to get to the year 2021.

Now in this present day world, she stood behind a person at the coffee shop with a desire to electrocute them all. It was against the eighth amendment of the United States to make her wait for coffee. She had a genuine need for coffee. She has, on more than one occasion, electrocuted someone for getting in between her and her coffee. These people in front of her were viewing this as some type of recreation activity, in which they were 'unsure' of what to get. Order the first thing that sounds good and get out of her way! She had seven meetings today, and then a flight to China to check out her warehouses there. Taking over companies in hostel take overs, though fun and exciting, always gives her too much work after the fact.

After what seemed like forever, she finally got to the front of the line. She saw it was the normal person and just gave him a look.

"ONE JUMBO EXTRA BLACK COFFEE WITH A SPLASH OF ALMOND MILK, NOW!" He yelled back to the baristas. "It will just be a moment, Doc. Busy today with holiday shopping. You are up next."

"Thank you, Jamie." Etain responded, putting down a fifty-dollar bill. "Keep the change." She moved to the side just as her coffee came up, and she took that first sip of ambrosia. She moaned, seriously. Once she had discovered coffee, she was sure that she would have been subdued by the heroes if they just put a pot of coffee in front of her. That is how much she loved coffee.

She sat and enjoyed the first cup, going through her emails, but pulling up videos of the one she kept an eye on over all these years. The only one that still played in her mind. Even with her steel trap of a mind, so many names and faces blurred over the course of four thousand years. But, still to this day, there was a grounding force to the one being that she cannot shake from her thoughts. She knew the person would never allow her to be in their lives. But Etain needed to know they are alive. Needed them to ground her, even if they never knew it. For they kept Etain safe from the monsters inside her head when they got too loud at times. Though nothing saved her fully. She had been broken and patched herself together with the pieces of her mind and soul left behind by those who had broken her soul.

She checked on them, then went and ordered another coffee, leaving another fifty dollars and left to go to the office. Evil never slept. Never a truer statement uttered, besides William Shakespeare once stating in his play, Hell was empty all the devils are here. Maybe that is what villains truly are, damned souls. For there were times Etain swore her soul was damned. She shook off the deep thoughts as she speed through the streets of Manhattan and slide into her parking spot. She took a deep breath and put her mask up and the Queen of Evil went to her day job.

CHAPTER SIX
IT ALL FALLS APART

Etain sat at her desk. There was so much paperwork now. There was so much work to do all the time. But it was worth it. VilCorp was the leading company of the world. It took secret meetings. Sex. Drugs. But then she found the answer.

She found the way through religion. Seems organized religion can brainwash even villains. She used their beliefs to turn them, and then about three hundred years ago when they went live, two hundred years after agreeing, she bought the higher ups in all religions. Humans tend to listen to their spiritual leaders. If she had their ear, then she had the ear of humanity.

Except for the atheists. She liked them, though. Anything she did that was not liked, was because of their own beliefs and thoughts. Not what they were told to think. As much as it made it harder to convince them at times to do what she wanted, those who thought for themselves were amazing beings.

It was not all those that followed a religion that were sheep, but the ones with their own thoughts were few and far between.

Plus, there was the fact she had her own cards she never showed even the people she was in business with; she was not going to get burned.

Her beliefs held close to her chest.

Her 'religion' never discussed.

If this all failed, and it went down in flames, she had to have a back-up plan.

She realized even if she got an agreement to a partnership; they were all villains. And could not be trusted.

Ever.

Always prepare for the worst.

And let the enemy burn.

She snorted to herself. There was corruption in everything. She watched as the many religions became more and more corrupt. And the leaders were crazy. Especially the Catholic religion. There was even a Pope that had all the penises removed off the statues because he did not like them, and now two hundred years later he has historians running around pinning dicks on the statues.

She stood and looked out the window of her skyhigh office. It was gorgeous in the night. The darkness calmed something in her soul. She could never be fearful, like many were of the dark. Darkness and evil may surround her soul, but she was well aware of the spark of light in the core. Much like the stars were specks of light in the darkness of the sky. She looked out and was satisfied. Content. But Etain was bored. Again.

Maybe she just needed sex. She stopped taking steady lovers after she got rid of John Lackland. And only had the occasional one-night stand. She blamed the stupid, gorgeous Phoenix. Ever since she started getting reactions from Phoenix, she felt like she was cheating on her when she had a steady lover. Yes, sex. That was all she needed. She went to the closet she kept at the office. One never knew when a dinner party or something came up and she would need an outfit.

She got dressed in her best clubbing clothes and stormed out the office. She had to forget the shit that went on in the boardroom today. Always the arguing. Different ways of bringing the company higher and higher. They looked to her for ideas, for guidance, to fix everything. And it was both boring as well as exhausting. She talked a good game for thousands of years. But honestly, she had nothing figured out. She had her demons buried so deep the only way she could function was to be the villain of the story. She just took one day at a time. Even four thousand years could not alter the fact she did not have it all figured out. She could only focus on what was in front of her and do her best to ignore the demons of her past. But rather she fucked up, failed, or won on this one day, she always woke up and prepared for battle every day. That was the only thing she could count on. That warrior within her soul. She got into her fast, fancy sports car, she pressed a button on her phone and Bohemian Rhapsody came on, and started to hum the opening. She adored that song. She pulled up to the club, singing the song at the top of her lungs. She grabbed her phone and threw her keys to the valet. It was time to party.

Etain went right in the club, went to the bar and grabbed a bottle if tequila. After drinking half the bottle, she went right to the dance floor. She grabbed a woman that Etain knew had a minor Earth power, as she worked for VilCorp, who was dancing with her lover and basically danced with her as if they were having sex with clothes on still. The lover took offense and got up in her face as he grabbed his girlfriend.

"She is mine. Go find your own slut!"

Etain turned, and her face grew cold. "You don't get to call her that. And you don't own her. She is with me tonight unless you don't want your job."

"Who do you think you are?" This brute of an idiot spat out at her.

"I am Bridget 'I am your fucking boss' O'Brien." Maybe she really should see a shrink about always using a version of her father's name as her last name. He no longer owned her.

"You are…" the lover sneered. "You are a bitch."

"Darling, I am the bad guy." She smirked and pulled his girlfriend in for a kiss. She then pulled the woman with her. The woman was bewitched and was more than willing. After all, as the world knew, even for a bad guy, her only set of morals was do not mess with kids and all sexual partners had to be willing.

Etain owned this club, and soon they were alone in a VIP room where Etain pushed the woman against the wall and ravaged her mouth. Pretending this golden russet skinned beauty beneath her was Phoenix, hoping an orgasm would at least give her a moment of feeling something other than monotonous existence.

Etain left the room, leaving her conquest. For the few hours she was with the woman, whose name she did not know, she could pretend that she was not alone. She sent an electric shock through the woman's brain. It would do no good for her to remember exactly who she had been pleasuring for a few hours. Mostly because she did not want to deal with drama at work, especially when all she wanted was an orgasm to forget how alone she was, and how much her dream was backfiring against her. She walked out of the VIP room, leaving a massive tip for the people who cleaned the room and for the valet, after all, if one did not tip then they were a waste of life, and out of the club getting into her car.

When she got home, she got ready to take a shower, grabbing a bottle of pills from the cabinet. She took three, ignoring the two maximum warning. She was just happy they stopped grounding up the bones of mummies and then selling them as a cure. She snorted; for so long humans were cannibals before condemning the practice. Medicine had come a long way. However, she missed the coke in Coke. She took her shower and crawled into her cold bed, wishing, and not for the first time, she had a certain hero by her side.

The next day she was sitting in her office again, sipping on her coffee. She had stopped at her normal coffee house and told her caffeine cleric to give her enough caffeine to run a minor planet. Etain was not sure what it was, but something about caffeine settled her, and she could never have enough. She believed that this was the greatest discovery of the world and anybody who can function before having coffee was more dangerous than herself, and she was evil incarnate, and needed to be destroyed. She had her computer on and a satellite on a small town in the middle of nowhere United States. Sometimes, she regretted immigrating to the United States back in the 1600's, but she was not about to allow Phoenix to come to this savage, blood thirsty land on her own. What was Etain watching on the screen? The answer was simple: she was watching Catriona.

Again.

Once VilCorp started up and the heroes started hiding or dying out, Etain never stopped watching Catriona. She always had eyes on her. From having minions protecting her in whatever place of this bloody land she settled in, which for the last sixty years had been in the middle of Iowa. She even sent gifts every so often. And since online shopping, it was simple to hack into her account and buy what she wanted and make it seem like she bought it with a gift card. Meaning, she could not figure out they were from her. Creepy and stalker-like, yes. But, she never planned on actually seeing Catriona in person again. Though, she wondered if the Greeks were on to something about humans once created to have two faces, four legs, four arms, and then were split and humanity spent their existence searching for the other half. She wondered if Catriona was her other half, opposite, but perfect for her. Then she would remember she was the bad guy and Catriona deserved the best. And though she was the best at being evil, she was sure not good enough for Catriona.

Etain knew that her little Phoenix was no damsel in distress. She knew Phoenix, though a gentle and loving person, was not weak. But she also knew that villains could not be trusted. Dibs was dibs, but sometimes villains... Well, villains are murderous, lying, untrustworthy bitches. She knew this because she was a villain. It was just like heroes were saving, trustworthy, martyr-type saints, that may or may not actually just have hero complexes. Seriously, some of the heroes just became heroes for the fame when they were famous. They got a hard on being able to save the people from the villains. She knew of at least a few, before they were betrayed and killed, that had a deal with villains to attack a town, the hero would get paid, they would run the villain off, and then they would split the gains. Almost always though the hero ended up killed, or at least sold out, by the devil they made their deal with for the silver coins.

Silver coins. She still used that turn of phase. She remembered when the first Christians tried to convert her. Though Jesus sounded like a hero more than anything, she always believed her powers, her life, her existence was born from the Earth. She worshiped nobody, but believed there was a godlike being, and she was a bitch.

After all, life was a double-edged sword. For each moment of contentment there were a million of pain and misery. She never worshipped this god, she did not really understand religion. How could anybody preach hate? She made her living off being evil, but she would never hate someone for being who they were made to be, because if everybody was made in this god's image, then even this god could make mistakes that mortals and semi-immortals have to fix.

Etain looked up as there was a knock on the door. In walked James, he had wanted to be a hero, a warrior, six hundred years ago, and became the villain due to greed. "James."

"Ah! Arc, sorry I can never remember the name you go by, I am still unsure why you never gave up your actual name. What with the villains running the world, thanks to you! Queen of Evil!"

"Because you don't trust a villain, even those in your debt. And the name currently is Bridget O'Brien. What did you need, James?"

"Board meeting tomorrow. A few of us got together. We have a plan to make this world more like we want it. Instead of controlling the ordinary people with now powers, and even the lower-powered beings, through our technology, perhaps we can control their very existence. Details will be given in the meeting."

"Very well, I will be there, of course, I still am majority stock holder. Wouldn't the world be shocked that corporate life and stocks were all created by a meeting of villains five hundred years ago!" Etain gave an evil, yet very fake, laugh.

James chuckled, "see you tomorrow, Arc!"

Etain stood in her house. She knew something big was going to go down soon. She could feel the charge in the air. Her life was going to change. She did not know how she felt about it, honestly her life was dull. She sighed as she opened the fridge. Food would be something to settle her.

She had papaya, calamari, granola, rainbow char, parsnips, and a bunch of colorful peppers. Calamari tacos with papaya salsa it was for dinner. She zoned out while she was cooking. She was distracted more and more by her own thoughts, to be honest.

She could feel the charge building for this coming change for a long time. Though the feeling was foreboding, and change was not always good, she was looking forward to change.

The last few centuries have been dull. She missed Catriona, also known as the Earth Phoenix. Life was exciting, even if she had always ended up licking her wounds and letting Catriona win. After all, some of the times, okay, most of the time, she let Catriona win, just so she could battle her another day. She had a feeling that Catriona was holding back as well.

She missed flirting with her. The last time they battled had been the most entertaining. She missed the battling! She never thought she would miss that give and take of the villains and heroes! She always wondered what it would be like if neither of them held back. What if they gave each other everything?

Another thought fleeted through her mind. Would she have stopped being the villain for Catriona? She would never be a good and moral person. She has done too much evil to ever be considered good. What if that girl she used to be, that girl who wanted nothing but a simple happy life, was still buried beneath the layers and walls she had built around her soul and heart?

It had been fear. Plain and simple. Fear that she would not be accepted. Fear that she could never find her way back. After all, she was over four thousand years old, and she had become the villain in her thirteenth summer. Nobody could come back from that evil.

She sat down with her dinner in front of her, her fancy long dinning room table spread out in front of her. How fitting… A table for a good two dozen souls; and she sat there alone at the head of the table. No love to her left. No right-hand person who she could trust. No friends. No family.

Oh, she never wanted children. That had never been in her plans, even when she was a young girl. That had been the dream of her first loves. She would have had her heir or heiress, but she would have taught them to be independent. She would not have been a warm mother.

She, even then, wanted power.

Wanted to change the way the world worked.

Change the course of humanity.

But under it all, she was still human.

She wanted a partner.

No, she wanted her Phoenix.

But that would never happen.

So, once she finished dinner, she went to her office and started to plan on expanding VilCorp once more.

For what she wanted, she would never get.

The Queen of Evil wanted to be loved by the Hero.

CHAPTER SEVEN
THE PAST IS MISSED

Etain sat at her desk. A novel in front of her. Thoughts of the past and her actions playing through her mind. 'She loves me. She loves me not.' Etain always figured it was about their creator and the fact one moment they loved the world. The next they regretted humanity existed and wished they never had created them. Which was why Etain believed that the creator just gave up, abandoned her creations and went her own way. And allowed each being to live in a version of damnation. Modern humans called it hell. Etain was in hell. People think that an endless existence was the dream. But as a practically immortal, Etain could tell them all that it was a punishment. Yes, she got to see the world change. She got to learn languages and watch as humanity evolved. She had got to witness firsthand exciting points of history. But, it hurts to exist. It hurts to be human. It hurts to hide it all under a mask. Humans did not get to choose to exist. Their parents made that choice. Then from the first breath, it is a fight to survive.

Oh, humanity will make life sound so pretty, especially when it is not. Humanity was a resilient sort of species. Without those who ground people, they lose it. Look at Etain herself. She lost the people who grounded her, and she became a mutherfucking supervillain that ruled the world. It was Etain against the world. Nobody had her back. But some sometimes she wishes her life had not turned out like this, as she was in what humanity called hell.

This hell she had created for herself. She had seen too much. She could feel a change. Something was happening in the world. A shift was coming. Something was breaking. The signs were all around. She had seen too much in this life to know notice the signs. She had seen evil bow at an altar, and she had seen the holy inside a bar.

Etain fell asleep at her desk. She did not know what the board meeting would bring, but she knew something in the world had to give. She almost welcomed the disturbance she could feel in the air. At least, it wouldn't be boring. Also, at least her dreams were of the past.

Etain had picked a fight. She could not help it. With VilCorp going live in just a few weeks, she wanted one last battle. One last chance to see her beautiful arch-nemesis. They had been battling for a while, at least a few hours, and Etain did not feel like letting Catriona win so easily today.

"If you want me come," Catriona panted out, it had been three hours of none stop battling and it was now the Devil's hour. "Come and get me." She stood, but swayed.

Etain paused and smirked. She rubbed the sweat and blood from her face and kept her hand upon her chin as if in thought. "Want you in what way, Angel? Don't get me wrong, both involve ropes, but it is an important distinction to make before we proceed."

Catriona blinked, "what on this forsaken Earth do you mean?"

"Think about it a moment Angel, what else could I do while I had you tied down?"

Catriona's eyes went wide, and she sputtered. "You think I mean sex?" She dropped the tree limb she had been using. "I can't have sex with a villain! I am a superhero! It would mean giving into you super villain! I can't have sex with a villain!"

Etain moved closer, "you are a woman, Angel. That means you can give into any sin you want. Including the sin of lust, even with a villain. Maybe we can even dye some of that hair of yours. Your black base with the Royal Blues, maybe some Violet for that Pride of yours." She was right up close to her, her own powers discharged for the moment. "Come on, Angel, join me in the Sins. Join my side. Become my Queen." She unleashed her powers. Allowing the electric charges to fill the surrounding air.

Catriona gasped, she saw the Wrath Red, Lust Royal Blue, Sloth Sky Blue, Gluttony Orange, Greed Yellow, and Envious Green. All of them mixed black, black of her soul, but under all that black was a white, like this villain used her darkness, used her sins, to hide they hurt her, hide her pure soul. It made Catriona swallow. Etain in her full glory was gorgeous. She backed up and her back hit the wall.

Etain smirked as she sauntered towards her and pinned her between her arms. "See what you could become? Come join me, Angel." She brushed her lips against her skin. "You are a woman. You can do what you want. You are a free agent. You can have it all. Even this empire of mine. You can have anything you want. You can do anything you want. I cannot be more than a villain. I will let you down if you try to change me. But…" Etain smirked and whispered into her ear, letting her lips touch the ear. "You can just be more than a superhero. You can be a Queen."

Catriona swallowed hard and pulled her power around her and disappeared. Never had she been so tempted to abandon good then she had been at that moment in time.

Etain pouted, but turned away from the damage and smirked. Soon, her view of ruling the world would come to fruit. And she could work on gaining her Queen over the coming centuries. She went back to her lair and her minions.

"Queen, what is next?"

"That was the ending battle. Pity. Of course, she doesn't flirt back." Etain sat on her throne and pouted.

"Queen?"

"I mean, just last month, I went and caused a non-lethal earthquake! I even made sure that nothing that but aftershocks hit the center of the village! I wore my tightest suit! I flirted. I suggested! And even today, I was very clear in how I wanted to worship her!"

A minion cleared their throat, "have you tried talking to her, Queen?"

"Huh?"

"You know, tell her you want her on your side. That you want her as your Queen Consort."

Etain blinked, "No, that would not work. She is too much of a hero. She would never change to being a villain."

"Maybe you could change?"

"No. I was made this way. I make no apologies for how I have become to protect myself." She clapped her hands. "So, minions! I think a new hell for ordinary mortals, jobs in 'customer service'. Basically, they would handle customers after we sell them our goods! Hell on Earth! Put them in tiny offices to answer letters, have them man our shops, and best of all, we don't have to deal with angry ordinary people!"

"Brilliant, Queen!"

"And it is time to buy the churches. People love religion." Etain rolled her eyes. She may believe that there was a creator, but she also believed that creator was a hands off mother type figure.

Etain woke up. She always wondered how Catriona reacted to that last battle.

Catriona had gone to bed later than normal, caught up in her newest cakes. One for the United States Thanksgiving. She still was not completely sure why they celebrated the start of genocide against the Native Americans, but it did give her a boost in business The Thanksgiving one was a Ginger Spice Cake using mainly ginger, the other spices were nutmeg, cinnamon, clove, star anise, and pink peppercorn, this one would have a Cranberry, Ginger, Nutmeg, and cayenne compote filling, and to cover it would be an American buttercream. The other was a special order for Christmas from a young woman who wanted to honor her family. It was to be three tiers. It will be an Irish Cream Peppermint cake with a dark chocolate espresso buttercream. The bottom tier would have little human figures made from sugar cookies with little macaroon drums. The middle tier would be a Nativity Scene, made out of chocolates flavorings will be white chocolate with spiced cherry filling, milk chocolate with a candied ginger caramel, and Dark Chocolate with spiced raspberry filling. These figures would be painted a pure white with a shine to look like porcelain. And the top tier would be the Three Wise Men following the Star with three gifts done as petit fours, the petit fours will be an almond cake with a fig compote. And the grand topper would be the Little Drummer Boy made from sugar. Maybe it was the late night, or the sugar, but something had her dreaming of Arc and the past.

Catriona landed in her home. She took deep breaths. She had to calm down. The temptation that was Arc had never been so hard to say no. She looked at her wall. Upon it was painted 'Do No Harm.' It was the code she lived by. It did not mean she rolled over and took Arc's shit. No, she fought back. But unlike with other villains, something held her back from defeating Arc. Something in her held back from causing more than a few broken bones and some stitches. She had lived by the code of being good, being the hero, since her mother discovered she had powers and made sure she knew right from wrong. She was hundreds of years old. Almost a thousand. Yes, Arc was older. One of the oldest, actually, but how could that darkness tempt her so? When all her life she had lived by a motto to protect, to harm no mortal, and fight the darkness in the world? Catriona never had been so tempted into allowing Arc to show her what she meant by ropes and sex. Catriona was no blushing virgin, but sex was not her thing. But now, in the darkness of her mind, her thoughts went to what if she gave into Arc? What if she stopped being the good guy? Would this desire be enough to turn into love and balance them? No longer the hero and the villain but a normal happy couple whose biggest fight was whose turn it was to take out the garbage? Catriona felt guilt over her thoughts, but she did not want to be the hero anymore. She wanted a rest. She wanted to live a quiet life. But Arc kept her from disappearing. Arc, and their battles, were the highlight of her existence. Catriona moved to take a shower and tried to push the thoughts of giving into Arc to the back of her mind. After all, she was the hero and Arc would never give up being the Queen of Evil.

Catriona woke up in a gasp. It had been so long since she entertained those type of thoughts about Arc. But even she had to admit she kept an eye on Arc. She was the CEO of the world's oldest and largest corporation. No matter the disguise, no matter the name changes, Catriona would always know Arc by her eyes. Those icy cold, electrical current blue eyes. Eyes that haunted her dreams at the most inconvenient times. She got out of bed; she knew she would not be able to sleep any longer.

Damn Arc and being in her darkest desires even hundreds of years later.

And damn her for not trying harder to destroy those thoughts.

For she still wondered if she could one day be shown all of Arc's desires.

She still wondered what it would be like to hang up the cape of being the good guy, rebel, join the winning side, and gain Arc all to herself.

She shook her head. It was selfish. She knew one day it would all get too much, and she would allow herself to no longer exist.

She could not lie to herself, it was Arc existing that kept her on this mortal realm.

As long as the Queen of Evil existed, there at least needed to be one hero out there that could fight her if needed.

And Catriona was the only one who ever held her own against Capitan Arc.

Now if the villain in question did not make her question her morals every time she saw her, then maybe she could have helped prevent the end of an era of superheroes and villains.

She moved to the kitchen. She would work her guilt out on her bread dough.

CHAPTER EIGHT
A VILLAIN NEEDS A HERO

Etain looked at the news. They kidnapped a child. She never understood why people wanted to hurt the innocent. They all did. Flamel with the stone used the blood of a thousand infants, or about two hundred liters of pure, innocent blood. Of course, Flamel did not get to use his horrific stone. Etain had made sure of that. She had hunted them down and drowned them in their own blood. After all, if they wanted to drain the innocent of their lifeblood, to take their souls, then it was fitting they drowned upon their own blacked soul source. Etain decided perhaps a bit of a detour was in order this morning.

It did not take Etain long to find out where they were. Stupid people using technology for everything. And she was not law enforcement, so she did not need a warrant. She broke into their place and had them shocked and down on the ground and tied up. She found the little girl and smiled. "It is okay, sweetie. Let's call the cops to get your mom and dad." She took out the phone and dialed 911. "Yeah, I found your missing girl. She is alright at this time. But I suggest getting to 915 Watercress Drive shortly, or I may have to do something terrible to the kidnappers." She hung up and looked down at the child. "No, I have to go. You will be safe. They won't wake up for a long time." She patted the kid on the head and turned and left just as the cop cars pulled up.

She should have killed them. But that brought questions. This way they will just leave her be. And right now she had more important things to do, like stop at her accountant's and lawyer's offices.

Today was a board meeting. They wanted to pitch something to Etain. What it was, she was not one hundred percent sure. Never before had they been so secretive. They must not think she would like it. She figured at some point they may do a coup. She had contingency plans. But, she figured it was at least a couple hundred more years off. To this day, eighty percent of the company's ideas were hers. Then again, she also knew villains were quite unpredictable. So she would proceed with caution. She also made sure she had ways out if needed. She had prepared to sell every single share. Every single one would crash the company. She could destroy what took a thousand years to build in moments. The others had sunk everything into this company. She made sure of that. Oh, they had their accounts hidden in tax shelters, but she would drain those at just the right moment. She always knew about them. And she made sure the best hackers in the world had taught her before she killed them.

She was a bad guy. But some of those hackers were worse. Yes, she took lives, yes; she destroyed things, but what she never did was leave someone alive to live in the torture of losing everything. Either by taking all their money and properties, or by creating false images and allegations against them. That was worse than taking their lives. She still had lines she would not cross. She just hoped she never got to the point she would cross the lines she had allowed herself to become blind to from the other villains over the years.

Etain came in laughing with a few of the other villains, some she had known for a thousand years. She was the oldest living gifted being. Gifted. How they used different words for the same thing. No more division of villain and superhero. Others had been killed off, or gave up and turned their powers on themselves, ending their extended life. Others just disappeared into the world. She kept an eye on most of them. But most were below her notice. The only one she kept an eye on with any regularity was Phoenix. Etain never really understood how she got that name. Arc, she understood. They named her for the arcs of her power. But a being that rose from the ashes? That had to come from her mother. She came from being a low being who would have been nothing but married off and bred to a hero. So, perhaps that is where her mother got the name Earth Pheonix.

"I am telling you, you will love the plan Etain."

"I am sure if it is feasible this meeting will be quick, Jerome."

"Oh, I am sure it will be." He smirked and took his seat.

Etain smiled as she took the head seat. "I call this meeting to order, Jerome, Richard, and James, you have the floor."

With that, the three stood up to pitch their plan.

Etain stood at the head of the table and looked at her board. "What the hell are you talking about?"

"Bridget, think about it for a moment."

"Think about what? You are talking mass genocide We make our living off the ordinary mortals!"

"But this way we would control the powered. You know we don't use our powers any longer. Many of our powers are weak, and those born with powers now are the weakest they have ever been, even compared to the first. If we got rid of the ordinary born, we can breed just those with powers. Then the powers would grow again! We can use them without fear. Without thought. Without hate!"

"Look, I am as evil as the next. But what you are talking about is killing the world. We can't run the fucking world if it is destroyed!"

"Not the world, Arc. Just those that are… ordinary. Wouldn't it be better if we had control of all those with power? That there were no ordinary humans to be offended they don't have power."

"Destroying all life is not the way to run a world! When I created VilCorp it was to have power. It was to have control! And we did that! I will have no part of this! And neither will this company! I still am a majority stockholder!"

"Bridget, we can do this with our without you."

"You will do it without my company! I put this together, I can tear it apart!"

A board member named Richard spoke, "the next stage of the world is imminent, why not join us in it?"

"I will not allow this! If we don't have ordinary people, then there will be wars once more. I will not stand for this, for if I am to fall, I am going to fall for what I believe in."

"We can't allow that Arc, it is why we drugged your coffee."
James smirked as he stood. He snapped his fingers, and a set of
minions walked in, some with minor powers of strength. "Kill her."

Etain went to shock them. She had not let it be known she still
exercised her powers, but did not want them to know how strong she
was. She could now feel the drugs flow through her system. But she
would be damned if she did not fight back. A small electrical current
went through the tables, chairs, and floor. But the contract was still
in place until the first minion of one of the other council members
touched her. "Fuck." She took off in a run. She had to at least get
out of the building. The only thoughts running through her head were,
how did they come up with this? She had worked hard to protect her
mind. She had created an electrical field around her mind, so the mind
readers would not get into her thoughts. How had they done this? If
they had not heard her darkest thoughts? If they had not heard a plan,
she threw away to make sure Phoenix never truly hated her enough to
kill her.

The minions gave chase once they were about five hundred feet
from the building they caught up with her due to the drugs running
through her system. They grabbed her and when she fought back, they
let their fists and feet fly.

Etain would not give up. She did not let anybody break her, since
her own father broke her mind. She fought back. She kicked. She
punched. She used what power she could, which was still stronger than
theirs, but with the drugs flowing through her system, was not strong
enough to kill them. No matter what drug in her system, she would
fight.

Etain did not know how long she fought back. She did not know how
long the battle was. She shocked them, but it was weak due to the
drugs. She broke some necks; she did manage to kill a few of them, but
they got her to the ground.

She did the only thing she could think of; she faked dead. She
brought an electrical current around her and made it appear as if she
had died. If they touched her, they would feel nothing but shocks
coming off her body. Checking for a pulse or heartbeat with tech would
just short circuit it. Not that she was not far from death, the
closest she had been in a long time. She could heal, but she would
have to sleep and allow the Earth's current heal her.

A minion came up and kicked her still body. "Think she is dead?"

Another kicked her again. "Yeah. We did what we were supposed to
do. No person could take a beating like that, and we shot her like a
dozen times.

"Do we take her back to the boss?"

One minion looked at the body, took his gun and shot her in the
chest. "Nah, she is dead. Let's go."

It took a lot not to scream out in pain from the gunshot.
Thankfully, she always wore a thin bullet proof material lined in her
clothes. That did not stop the pain of the pressure of the bullet hit
her chest. She could practically feel her internal bleeding. She had
to get to the one person who could help her. The one person who was
still a hero.

Catriona.

She started to crawl. It was only a matter of time before she took the fall. She found the river where she kept a boat. There was a reason she ran this way. She always kept backup plans. She never trusted. But it was time she laid all her cards on the table. It was time to give a hero all her keys.

She saw this coming. She knew her choices and Karma would catch up to her, eventually. Her pain could only allow her to do so much evil. Now she would have to sink to her knees and beg for help from the one person she could never stop thinking about, even after a hundred and sixty years of her retiring from being a hero.

Etain got to her boat; she looked at her minion that was mind controlled by a shock collar she put on them. "Go to the following coordinates. 42°22'00.6"N 92°45'44.1"W. Then you will kill yourself and burn the boat." It would be a blessing at this point to be killed. Their mind controlled for too long. Etain winced. She just hoped her hero never found out about that way of controlling people.

"Yes, Queen." The minion started the boat as Etain crawled below.

Etain looked out the window at the side of her bed. She could not sleep, or she risked not waking up. Would Catriona listen to her? Would she hear her call for help? The question that came to her mind was, could Catriona save her from the damnation of Dubnos?

Etain knew she would not heal until she slept, but she could not sleep, not until she got to Catriona. Using the rivers and creeks to get to where she was would take a week, even with the high-speed boat that she owned. She made sure to get up and move, small cat naps to keep the internal bleeding at bay, and protein shakes to keep her energy up; but she had her minion wake her from those naps.

As she traveled to the one that may be able to help her, she looked out into the darkness and she wanted to scream. She could not get the scream from her throat. Anger, hurt, pain, weakness, grief. These emotions threatened to drown her.

But through it all, that flicker of light still in her dark and damaged soul was whispering out two words.

The piece of her soul reaching out to the one she was fighting to get to.

The words: HELP ME.

And that whisper is what gave Etain the power to continue on her journey.

During that week, Etain kept working on her arguments to get the hero to help her. She went through all the standard; she was the hero bullshit. But nothing sounded like it would work. She decided she would actually have to tell the truth.

If it would help her case, Etain knew she would give up her throne to Catriona to help her save the world. She snorted every time that thought went through her head. Queen of Evil fighting to save the world. But Etain had faith in her hero. But she also knew her hero would need proof that Etain was honest in her request, and the only way to prove she was telling the truth would be to give the truths. To give her name. To give her story.

She had never been in this situation. She was never one to need help. She now had to swallow her pride to ask for help. If there really was a God, Etain hoped She was listening to her request. She had always known there was The Goddess, but Etain was sure that The Goddess abandoned Earth long before even Etain was born.

Etain also knew if she was still capable of love, she might be in love with Catriona. But all Etain had learned from love in the past was that it would rip her heart for her soul and leave a giant gaping wound where her soul's heart once was, had she not learned that lesson when she last gave her heart almost four thousand years ago?

CHAPTER NINE
EVIL EXPOSED

James smirked as his minions came back and told them they left her body in the woods, shot in the chest too! If found, the cops would just think she was attacked and shot by a random person. This town was dangerous. It is one of the reasons that that the fourteen villains convinced Arc to move them to this dangerous town. Before the last century or two, most of the villains stayed in Europe, while Arc was over in the colonies and new world.

James was glad that Arc had ran to the new world. Why she left, they never figured it out, but when she left Europe, she turned a blind eye to all the evil they did to people. She would keep them somewhat informed of her movements. She joined the military many times in her life. She always said it satisfied her need for battle and chaos. Where the fourteen others were happy having power and money, which was the reason they became villains to begin with, Arc always needed adventure, battles, chaos, and to be constantly moving.

And now she was dead. Left with a bullet in her chest, after being beaten, in the middle of a park.

And best of all?

Nothing would come back on him or VilCorp. He sat down in his office. The only thing was that the moment she left the building, her office and labs were shut down and locked up. They had to figure out how to get into them. They tried blowing the door, but it had not worked. Then again, Arc had four thousand years of tricks up her sleeves. But thanks to a little drug made by a new doctor down in the labs, they finally got one over on the Queen of Evil.

The doctor came in at that moment. "Daniel! The drug worked perfectly."

Daniel chuckled darkly, "I knew it would. If you mix it with a bit of aspirin, they won't be able to even move. You could do anything with them."

"Pity I didn't know that tidbit. I would have had a bit of fun with her before I killed her."

"I came up here because, the labs locked down. The computers locked. Everything."

"Yes, we discovered. We are looking for someone who can hack her system. But if we do it wrong, it wipes everything out. As it is, somehow, and I don't know how, she sold ever last piece of stock in every single company. Made the Earth's weight in gold. And it crashed the market. We just lost billions. Well, it must be her computer system. She is dead. She always did have a plan."

"She did create VilCorp, sir."

"I know that, Daniel. She gave me my chance. But never trust a villain." James chuckled darkly as he turned to look at the statue out in front of the building. It was of Arc, of course, surrounded by bolts of electricity and showing the world her cold ice queen exterior. "She always was the best villain. And it took a century since we started this plan for her to become vulnerable."

"She is the oldest."

"Was. Now she is dead." James turned around. "The plan to wipe out the ordinary people?"

"Locked out. That is the problem. We can't start production until we are in. It will take us at least two months to get around their systems."

"Fuck. Fine. Go! Try to replicate it in the meantime. I will deal with the crash." James waved his hand and Daniel was smart enough to leave. James looked out at the statue. He really had wished he had known about the aspirin thing. Out of the fourteen other members, twelve were men, and they all had waited for the whore to want to fuck them. She slept with anybody she thought 'pretty', but said it was not good for business to sleep with the council. Of course, they would have had to kill her before she woke from their fun. Anybody who knew her as Arc knew she killed those who raped. With no mercy.

He pushed the thoughts away.

He looked towards the television that had been playing in the background. The reports coming in were not good for VilCorp.

The anchor was reporting on the crash. "Today in a shocking move, the O'Brien Heiress sold all her stock in VilCorp. And for the first time in the corporation's history their stock has crashed. Rumors are flying about a takeover or that the Heiress has found love and has decided to leave the country to their rumored private island to live out her days with the lover or lovers that finally got her to settle down. More on the O'Brien history and her scandals can be found on our website."

"David, if this was a takeover, she seemed to have an idea it was coming, as she sold the stock at the highest VilCorp has ever been. She literally made trillions with the selling of her stocks. Bridget O'Brien did not keep a single stock in VilCorp or any of the subsidiaries. She sold everything. So, I do not believe it was a hostel take over, if it was, she had plans in place in case she was betrayed by her once trusted board. If that is the case, VilCorp may finally come to an end after hundreds of years. As all patents are in the O'Brien name as well as the fact the O'Briens have been a trusted name in households for just as long. If they sold everything, and are walking away, VilCorp may just have to earn the world's trust once more. More tonight at ten!" The female anchor gave her opinion and basically put another nail in VilCorp's coffin. If James did not fix this, and soon.

James threw his glass at the television. He was pissed. He did not need this. He took a deep breath. He took another. He had a council to take control of, and the party was about to start at his mansion. He would just find some young thing and take his frustrations out on her or him. He moved and threw his suit coat on and walked out of his office. Time to celebrate!

James walked into his house. The party was in full swing. He saw a little young thing, probably barely legal. They were probably here looking for a sugar daddy. James had a few toys like that. He bought them trinkets, and then he used them for his release and pleasure. He made a lot of them wear certain clothes, shoes, even act a certain way. And the control he had over them, that gave him a rush even the power his money gave him could not buy.

But no, this one would not be one of his personal toys. He would use him, leave him in a puddle of his release. He would leave the door open and so anybody could walk in and use the boy. Minions waited for things like that. James knew Jerome was already in a bedroom. James moved over. Time to start the domination, taking the boy in the middle of the party before moving to a room.

Oh, how Arc would have killed them all if she ever had known about these parties.

Jerome walked out of the bedroom, his latest toy still on the bed. He waved his hands at his minions, saying they could have their go. He always did award his men. He looked to see James practically raping a young man in the middle of the party. Richard was drunk and had his wife sitting on his lap. Sometimes even he felt bad for that woman. To always have to have that man's dick in her.

These parties always brought out the worst in the villains. Well, they were the bad guys. Sometimes he wondered if it was the loss of their powers that made them more heartless.

Jerome was not a fool. Once VilCorp came to be, almost all stopped using their powers. They got their power another way and enjoyed the high it gave them. But they kept getting worse and worse, as their humanity seemed to disappear with their powers. Jerome was not a fool. He had noticed as they used their powers less, as they aged, as lost their powers, they became darker, eviler, and for damn sure more ruthless.

He moved and got a whiskey. He looked around at the other nine men on the council. They all had their 'dolls'. Jerome doubted that a single villain but Arc had a willing sexual partner. Those married had bought their spouse, raped them and forced them to marry them. or just taken them and broke them. They all felt power and money entitled them to anything. And they had the law in their pocket. Nobody reported what happened to them. Nobody ever spoke of these parties. The people would come for a good time, even a show. And most got that. Some, however, became the show, became the toy, and often disappeared after a party. Either through a cleanup, or they ran back to whatever small no name town they came from.

Yes, if Arc knew, she would have killed them all.. Not that they ever let on to Arc what they had been doing. Even the two women on the council had their pets. They were out in the hot tubs making their pets, who were truly in love with their owners, watch as they fucked anybody that came up and offered their body.

Richard had his wife sitting on his lap. He was no fool. He knew why she had married him. He had asked, asked, and asked some more for a date. Then when she kept saying no, he went abusive to her. It resulted in him raping her. She got pregnant and her father made her marry him. Now she had no life to her. She was a thing for his pleasure and to raise his children. Five years since the wedding and they had seven children. He was about to put another one in her belly soon. After all, now that the fourteen of them controlled VilCorp, he could hire a few nannies. Hot, young ones, after all, sometimes the body in his bed did not have enough fight to make him pleased.

He knew they had no souls. And he knew they had no humanity left. They all truly lost that when they chose to be the villains. Only Arc had a soul. A moral compass. How she had actually ever became as evil as she did, he did not know. They all had guesses. But in the end, nobody knew. She had killed. She had become so feared they called her the Queen. It was one of the reasons they listened to her to begin with.

However, now that he sits here basically powerless, he has to wonder: Did she do this to make them lose their powers? Had she planned her own take over? No. She did not use her powers either. He shook his head. Tonight was a celebration. They got rid of Arc. Soon the ordinary humans would all be dead. They would own the world. They could bring powers back to the world. Back to them. And they would be the rulers. Yes, he stood up and pushed his wife in front of him. It was time to move to a bedroom.

James found a nice young man to take his frustrations out on, and it had worked for a bit of time. But now that he was done with the man next to him, his mind started to work again. Arc had to have a password. An override. She lived and breathed VilCorp. Arc played her hand close to her chest. Always did. Not a soul in life knew her actual name. Not a soul alive knew her history. They all knew she was over four thousand years old, she had told them that much, and even the others who were in their thousands had stories of how Arc held the world hostage with fear. The only problem now was not trying to get close to her, not trying to charm her, may delay their plans by six months or more.

At least that was the text message he was looking at from his tech guy.

'J, her programs are insane. It will take me six months minimum to get through. Probably a year.'

'Force it?'

'You do that you lose everything.'

'Fuck'

'J, I will get it'

'You better. Or you will become a disposable.'

'Fuck you'

James did not respond. He sighed and got up. He walked out of his room to see most of the guest were passed out. He moved through his house and went outside to look up at the sky. He did that to think. There had to be something somebody knew that could help them get into the system. They had plans. But right now, if they still wanted to be more powerful, they needed to get ahead of the crash their stock took because of Arc's back-up plan.

"Fuck you, Arc." He stated to the air. Even in death, she was causing him issues and delays. He would show the world the Queen was dead, so Long Live the King.

CHAPTER TEN
THE RETIRED HERO

Catriona was kneading the dough for her bread. Thoughts of her dream still playing in her head.

She had retired when Arc won. Arc finally took over the world. Arc united the villains, and suddenly heroes had no cause. She turned to the television when an ad came on, a reminder of how the heroes failed.

"And remember, life without chaos is like a superhero without a cause. VilCorp will always be around to bring excitement and controlled chaos to life." Catriona blinked as the ad for a new theme park finished.

Nobody believed in true villains and heroes anymore. All heroes either died or some, like her, hide out in a mortal life. Even the villains did not show their powers anymore. Tales of villains and heroes battling for the soul of humanity were just fairytales now.

And in real life the bad guy won.

Catriona remembered how things played out. It was not right away. It was not quick. It was subtle.

At first Catriona, as well as other superheroes, thought that they had beaten back the villains as there were fewer attacks. Less death. Less… evil. But they would be proven wrong.

It would be too late to do anything once they learned what was truly happening. The heroes were sucker punched by the villains and the monsters under the bed came out into the light and convinced the world they were the ones to follow.

What was it about being evil that gave them a silver tongue?

Perhaps her mother had been right. That some souls are touched by the Fallen Morningstar himself, giving them his talents of silver tongue and controlling evil.

Catriona shook her head. No, she did not believe people were born evil. Arc was not born evil. No. Something broke her. Catriona had felt and seen that light of her soul being protected by the darkness of her sins.

Catriona blamed herself. She was so focused on 'playing' with Arc, that evil finally won. Catriona always seemed to be where Arc was wreaking her havoc. Still to this day that bothered the retired hero. It was like Arc stopped wanting to cause evil and play with Catriona. Arc still killed, but Catriona had noticed a pattern about those she killed. They were all evil themselves. Catriona said nothing about the pattern. Because with the destruction to the towns before Catriona started battling her, who would believe the hero that the villain was hiding under a villain mask?

After the first couple of battles, Arc started to just be a nuisance instead of a villain. Though with a murder here or there, people still saw her as a ruthless, heartless, soulless villain.

Arc did always seek Catriona out. They battled, Arc flirted. But Phoenix tried not to respond to that, though towards the end there was a lot of blushing. A lot of guilt that maybe if she had not been so busy flirting, she could have prevented VilCorp.

In the end, VilCorp opened, and the people cheered. They made life easier with their products. With their technology. Now they had their hands in just about everything from entertainment to government contracts. VilCorp controlled the way the world ran. They had money. Power. They won.

Catriona should have stopped her somehow. But she was weak. She fell for everything that Arc did for her. The sparks of kindness, even if it was only toward children or Catriona. Each gift Catriona should have said no, thank you, should have said no, should have denied it all. But after that first gift, after that first one, it became addicting. She was addicted to Arc's small sparks of kindness. Arc courted her and made her fall in love, all without trying. She gave in so easily to Arc. She should have been strong. But she was so weak. She loved Arc. And that was the reason she stayed in this quiet town, why she still hoped one day Arc would find redemption. Every time Catriona had said she would not fall again, Arc would show that damn heart of hers.

Oh, she knew those mystery gifts were from Arc. Letting the retired hero know that Arc still knew she was alive. Arc still knew where she was, and still was on the villain's mind.

She remembered the one time Arc was attacking a town, why Catriona could not say, but she was sure it was because the other Villain, Tic Tok, needed assistance and Arc was recruiting villains for her future company. Tic Tok had gone to kill a child, and Catriona had been too far away to save the child. Arc had gotten to him and had his throat in her fist. Catriona could hear what she said clearly, as if she was still living it.

"You never kill a child. Children are to be protected. Even from the likes of us. You just wrote your own death warrant, William." And with that Arc had sent her power through her hand and burned Tic Tok alive. She had dropped the body and went and checked the child before turning to Catriona. "What?"

"You killed your partner."

"He was not my partner. He was a tool to be used. But he proved I could not leave him alone and follow the laws of my alliance. He had to be put down like a rabid mutt." Arc landed in front of Catriona. "What? There are laws that even I won't allow to be broken. Not everybody is pure darkness. Just very, very close. Good bye sweet hero." With that, Arc disappeared, leaving Catriona to help clean up the town.

Catriona shook her head and ignored the memories. Each memory of bad always was destroyed in her mind when she would remember those sparks of kindness. Catriona sighed, she was still weak. Two hundred years since VilCorp went public. Five hundred years since the Villains became corporate, and still it was Arc that filled Catriona's waking and sleeping thoughts. She turned back to what she was working on. The bread would not knead itself.

Etain used all her strength as she ran to the only being she could trust. The flood waters were rising, the fires of hell were coming to Earth. Etain had been living in a glass house too long. She had lost her sight. She could no longer live in the shadows, no longer take comfort in the darkness of the night. It was the eleventh hour and the world now had to place all its faith in a woman who gave up being a hero a long time ago when Etain and the Darkness won. When Etain succeeded in causing the hero to give up being a hero. When Etain made the mistake in thinking that the world did not need the heroes whole the villains ruled. She messed up. She failed. She lost her vision of why she became the type of villain she had become, and let the power corrupt her fully.

She stopped caring. Turned a blind eye to her 'partners'. And for once, Etain was terrified it was all going to end. She did not know how they would get the world set straight again.

For centuries, Etain had dominated a world. She had all the power. She never needed a hero. She had taken care of herself. She had never had to call out for help. And now she needed someone to help her fight. She could only think of one being. The world was in danger, and Etain knew if the ordinaries were killed, it would break her sweet hero. Oh, she was not lying about needing them to rule for the power. But in all honesty, it was so it would not break Catriona's soul.

No matter how many how many centuries pass, since meeting Catriona, every action she had taken she calculated how it would affect Catriona.

And that scared Etain.

So fucking much.

But she kept pushing forward.

If she did not, all would be lost.

She finally made it to the little house. She fell against the door. She knew once that door opened, all lies would be lost. All masks would be dropped. Etain raised her hand. It was her last time to ignore what her soul was saying about trusting this hero. After this moment she knew when she woke she would have to finally face the past she was running from, as her hero would need the full truth. Without the truth, Etain would not be able to convince the retired hero to take her mantle once more. She took a deep, painful breath. She closed her eyes.. She let her hand fall against the door. For she knew, when the bombs were dropping, as the world was on the edge of annulation, there was only one she could trust.

"Catriona…" She fell against the door, barely conscious.

Catriona was getting ready for bed when she heard a thump against her door. She moved and put a robe around her to go to the door. She looked through the outside viewer and saw nothing. She frowned and opened the door. Nobody seemed to be there. She moved to go back in when a hand grabbed her ankle. She started and looked down. There was a bloody, hurt, and almost dead Doctor Arc.

"Help me…" Etain gasped. "Please, Catriona. Help." With that, Etain passed out. She had used the last of her strength to get to this small town in Iowa. To the only person her soul trusted. Even if she was a hero, that did her best to defeat her once upon a time. She knew that Catriona would answer the call once more to be a hero. Because she was a good soul, a true hero.

Catriona blinked and then jumped into action. She moved and went and got some blankets to help move Etain in, using more than a bit of her abilities to get her to a bed. Once Catriona got her to the bed, she blushed as she removed her clothes. But she had to get to the injuries. She signed as she saw the damage, helping set the bones, cleaning the cuts. The most concerning bruise was over her heart. A bullet had fallen from her clothes. As she removed them from Arc. They had tried to shoot her in the chest. Someone had actually tried to kill her. Catriona took a deep breath to calm the fury she could feel building within her. Arc had called dibs in Catriona. That went without saying, Catriona had dibs on Arc. Someone had tried to kill HER Arc! She took a deep breath. She had to help Arc now. Deal with the bad guys later.

Catriona took her time to fix what she could. She really only had basic first aid training, and her years of helping patch up the odd victim or herself after a battle. She put Arc in the guest room and her clothes in the wash. She sat down in her kitchen with a cup of tea.

The tables had turned. This time she was the knight in shining armour. Oh, she was no fool. Arc had more than once showed up in the eleventh hour and saved Catriona in the past. There were many times the villain should have won, but then Arc would show up and kill them. No thought, no care. When Catriona asked why, Arc would just smirk and say, 'I called dibs little damsel in distress.' There would be some flirting. Then Arc would disappear once more, often leaving a gift behind.

Catriona did not know what it was, but she always got a warm feeling when Arc would do things for her. Save a group of people, protect her village those few times villains attacked it when she was gone, and most of all, saving her many times. She wondered if Arc just did not know how to express her feelings. God only knew that Catriona practically fell in love with her.

And to tell the truth, Arc always did seem a bit… Well, on the Spectrum. Catriona had studied many things in the years, and psychology spoke of autism spectrum disorder. Under that was Asperger Syndrome, and as the years went by and Catriona thought of Arc, and watched her in her many personas, Catriona was sure Arc fit on the Spectrum.

One day, Catriona hoped to prove it.

But that was not a priority.

They only interacted as Arc and Phoenix, but Catriona had been tempted to seek her out as Catriona.

Oh, she knew Arc never went by her actual name, but it was not hard to figure out who she was going by, mostly because Arc would leave clues for her, before the time of television. After, well,, Arc appeared enough on television for VilCorp. If Catriona had needed something, somehow she would get it, and she ignored the signs, but she knew everything came from Arc. When her mother was sick and there was no way to get a certain medication because it had been outlawed as witchcraft, but then Arc turned up with a healer just days after Phoenix had let slip in battle her mother was sick and she did not have time for Arc's antics. Arc smirked, and told the Healer to do what Phoenix told them to do, or pay the price. Arc left, and Pheonix got thirty more years with her mother.

She could not lie to herself. She knew part of the reason she never took the route many heroes did, and let their powers, thus themselves, die, was because Arc was still there. Still in her life. Still leaving gifts. Like when she went to get the money for the bakery when she first opened it sixty years ago. There was no way she should have been approved for that loan.. And there was also no way that she won a contest that paid off the mortgage, after having said loan for only fifteen days. And the bakery should have gone under years ago, but somehow there were always big orders coming in, always more than enough to keep the doors open and Catriona living comfortably.

Catriona could not prove it, but those orders had to come from Arc.

Every time she stopped to think about Arc, her heart hurt that they were on opposite sides. If Arc would become neutral out of this, then she knew she would end up begging Arc never to leave her side. She was no fool. She did not have much to offer the Queen of Evil. Nothing to give her that could tempt her into giving up evil and living a quiet life with Catriona. She could just hope that after this Arc would never leave her alone again. Could this hero save the one soul that she wanted to be selfish enough to keep?

Catriona went and sat next to Arc. She hoped that Arc would heal. She hoped that when Arc woke up, she would finally have answers. And she would get the chance to keep the villain that stole her soul. Not that she could give any indication of that fact. She still had to figure out why Arc showed up at her door. Catriona would keep watch over Arc. She made herself comfortable in the chair and closed her eyes. Forbidden dreams of a quiet domestic life with Arc would play through her mind, as she begged a God she was not sure still listened, to heal the woman who had a hold on her soul.

CHAPTER ELEVEN
BEGGING

Catriona sat watching the villain she knew was Doctor Arc. Never had she seen this villain in the state that Catriona found her arch-nemesis, and they had been in some extreme battles. Honestly, Arc should have killed Catriona a long time ago. But Arc always let her get away, or she always quit and left. After spending most of the battle flirting. Speaking of tying her up. Speaking of bringing her to the most intense orgasms of her life. Catriona always ended up blushing. Arc had always been the only one she was tempted to even think about sex with. Other than that, Catriona had no desire for sex. Demisexual, is what they call it nowadays, for she had this connection with Arc, and she was sexually attracted to Arc. Somehow, and Catriona was not exactly sure how, Arc made that emotional connection with her. Their battles had just become major flirting sessions. An play, like the theater, where Arc pretending to destroy and Catriona pretending to defeat her.

When Catriona had been born, not being interested in sex, just made her a standard woman who, if she had not had her powers, would have been forced to marry and have children. Being a hero allowed her a freedom that many did not have in those times. However, she heard of the rumors around Arc. She was one who even told the world 'I like pretty people'. Though the rumors said if the person was powerless Arc would not give them the time of day.

But other than that, Arc was… very free with her body. Catriona tried to ignore the jealousy that built when she thought of Arc with someone.

There was also the rumor that disturbed Catriona, that since that battle with the volcano in the village over from hers, that Arc had not had another steady lover since breaking it off with Lord of Ireland John Lackland. Who just a year later became king when his brother was murdered. Catriona always wondered if Arc had something to do with that. But if she had, why did she not use that as a way to become Queen. After all, the entire world knew John was besotted to Arc, who at the time went by the name Katherine O'Brien. The world would not have been upset if King John had married Katherine O'Brien, the people of England believed she settled John Lackland. They loved her, no matter if they did not know her history. So, why not become Queen. But none of that was as important as one question.

The fundamental question in Catriona's mind, was how did Arc find her? Each and every time she moved, Arc found her. It would have to wait until Arc woke up. If she woke up. Her injuries had been pretty horrible, and Catriona did not know if Arc had a healing ability.

She prayed Arc woke.

It was almost two days before Arc woke up. When she did, she sat up with a start and looked around. Her eyes landed on Catriona. She sighed, in relief or frustration she did not know.

"Catriona." Etain croaked out and cleared her throat.

Catriona walked over with a glass of water. "Why did you come here, Arc?"

"I need help."

"Why me?"

"Catriona…"

"Answer me, Arc!"

"Because I need a superhero."

"Doesn't explain anything."

"Want a truth or a lie?" Etain was not good with truths, but would give it to this woman. She never really understood how this woman could get under her skin, when she never allowed any other to make her… emotional… even thinking the world made vile build up in the back of her throat. She had made sure emotions never played a role until this superhero with her perfect… everything.

"The truth if you know what that is."

"Hey! I can tell the truth."

"When it suits you."

"Okay, you have me there. But I am the bad guy." Etain gave a smirk through the wince of her still extremely tender ribs.

"Arc," Catriona growled.

"I dug my own grave. I mean, I knew that I would. Nothing lasts forever right, but I thought I had figured out the balance, you know? I helped kids. I helped you. But, in the end, I made my own bed, and I have no right to ask for help. But maybe you can help protect, not only this world, but this Icarus. I forgot I was not invincible."

"Arc…"

"Hey, we were a mess. I picked fights I could not win just to fight you. I knew where to find you because I kept an eye on you. Five hundred years and it never really was over. This hold you have on me. Even the only people I ever loved never had this much of a hold on me. Maybe, it is because you didn't kill me, even though you saw my dark side. So, I put up even more amour around my heart. I built my own wings to fly to the heavens. I built a damn company from nothing, gathered all the villains to stop the useless fighting. Destroyed the superheroes in one bloody, horrible, brilliant move. But there was always you there. You grounded me in your own way, even if I was only flying towards my own destruction. You and your… goodness, it…" She sneered, "it made me think of being, if not good, neutral. But, I thought I would literally become the Queen of Evil and I would stop thinking about you, the stupid hero that put stupid thoughts in my head of maybe changing. I had to rewire myself, I slept with more people than I can even count, ever since I made my choice. But somehow, through all my thousands of years, you made it through the armour."

"Why didn't you ever change? Why come to me?"

"It is a long way back from what I became. I am well over halfway to whatever damnation is waiting for me in death. You believe in…" she tilted her head; she was born in the early tenth century in the common era. "Hell?" At Catriona's nod, she continued. "I am over halfway to Hell. I have done so much evil. So, with that thinking, how could I ever make things right? I know I never killed an innocent, and my minions are far from innocent. They are murders, abusers, I control

them, then when their use is over I kill them. So, before you go down
that road, I never have killed an innocent. And I craved power. Power
to make sure I was never hurt again in this existence of mine. Why did
I come to you? Why am I going to ask you to fight a war? We were never
over. I left you with a billion questions, no answers. A pathetic last
fight, where I put the thoughts of lust and being maybe neutral, in
your mind. Be we never finished anything. You are my arch-nemesis, in
but name only, but we never were over. Do you know my proper name,
Catriona?"

"No, Arc. Considering I have been calling you Arc since you
finally woke up."

"Maybe it is time I explain how I ended up here." Etain sighed as
she laid her head back. "Why I can't change, why each time I thought
about it, why I tried to the line. I thought of her. Four thousand
years and my heart and mind still takes me back."

"Why you are on doorstep may be a good place to start." Catriona
sat down but kept tense, ready for battle.

Etain snorted, "I will not hurt you. If I wanted you dead, you
would have been killed a thousand years ago. All I have to do is send
out an electric shock to your heart. It is how most of those who beat
the shit out of me died. However, there are some who have a shield
against me. The whole council, actually. When we first made our
agreement, our contracts state we could not personally kill each other
but we can hire minions to do so. However, if caught hiring minions,
the protections are void. I can now kill them, but I have to get them.
That is where I need you."

"Look, explain to me why you want to take down your own
brainchild, or maybe give me your name since you know mine?."

Etain ignored the question about her name. She had long ago
stopped speaking it even in her own mind. She was either the mask she
created for the world or Arc. "I wanted children once upon a time, you
know. Well, not really. I wanted a marriage, an heir, a family. That
once my most selfish thought was that I would die before those I
loved? How selfish is that? That has got to be the most selfish
thought ever. To want to die first so I would not have to feel that
pain. But leaving them to feel that pain."

"What does that have to do with anything?"

"Let me explain. Most people have to look back and find that fork
in the road, find where it all went wrong. I don't. I know exactly
when I made my path. Not everybody has a clear fork in their path.
Normally it is little diversions off their path, little bit of take a
scenic route, and they have to look back and see it was not one big
thing, but a million little things. For me, it isn't like that. It was
one event, that led to me being the way I am. And I will explain this
to you."

"Well?" Catriona was getting impatient; and to hear that this
woman wanted a family meant she had been in love with someone, and
that just made her envious. To know there once someone that she choose
over power. Thankful her power did not spark with her strong emotions.
Not that she could show that this was Arc after all and could not be
trusted.

"It all started in the Bronze Age, and I was born Etain, daughter of Brian…"

Etain was happy, insanely happy. She had a way to have it all. Nobody knew she had a power. Nobody would take her simple life from her. Or so she thought. But of course one man was going to destroy her life.

Her father.

Yes, the man who was her sire, her father, if the man could be called that, discovered her sister had a power. It was not a major power; it was a simplistic power. She had a minor ability over the Air element and could move smaller things with the air. At that moment of discovery, their father 'sold' her sister to the clan leader to be his bride. Her sister had just been nine. Her sister had bled to death that 'wedding' night from the rape.

Etain exploded with her power when she found out. She and her girlfriend had been at the next village over, planning their wedding to the heir of the land in the village. In that time, the fact she had been thirteen and just getting wed was a bit late. She had come home to her mother crying. When her mother explained the marriage and her sister's death, Etain went to her father.

Her father said it was the way the world was. Women were nothing more but tools to have heirs and for male pleasure. And her sister had to have a power that was controlled. That she died showed just how weak she was, and she deserved death.

Etain exploded and used the electrical current of the Earth to kill her father and the man who raped and killed her sister. The clan leader had run from his hut, where he had been raping another woman. The blood still upon his hands and dick. She glowed with the electrical currents of the Earth and sent them through the men to fry them, allowing them to live until the pain and damage of their bodies caused them to internally bleed out and then, and only then, did she allow the nerves of the heart and brain to die.

When the other men tried to kill her, she killed them. When the air cleared, the ones who had been murdered by the men of the Clan Leader had included her girlfriend, her future husband, her mother, and many others from her village. She had turned to see very few of her village and the surrounding three still standing. She looked at her reflection in the lake. Her eyes had changed from warm chocolate brown to the bright blue of electrical currents. Her hair was blowing in a breeze that did not exist. She could still feel the currents. She could still feel how it felt to drain the life from these men. Men who had raped and killed many of the women born to this clan. She had been lucky. Her best friend's father had set up a marriage contract when they had just been children. Her best friend also enjoyed the company of other men to women. They were going to bring another man into their marriage, in addition to herself and her girlfriend. Multi-marriage households were common at this time, especially for families who owned the lands and resources.

She turned to those remaining, and with the last bit of emotion she had in her soul. "I am sorry." Etain ran the electrical current through the grounds to the remaining people who knew her name and killed them all. Then she stood there alone. They were not innocents.

They allowed a child to raped and murdered just because the man had the most resources.

She buried her sister by the rock that they had carved their names it.

Odd for the time, as most were burned to ash.

But she could not set fire to her sister.

She had nothing.

She did the only thing she could do.

She had run.

What more could she do? She no longer had a home. She no longer had anybody she cared about, loved.

So, she had run.

She would pop up in towns and when she heard of children brides, she killed the men. When she was eighteen she found she control men and women with sex. When she was about twenty, she found she had stopped aging. That the currents of the Earth fed her a life force that kept her young and immortal. So, she went through the time lines being a villain. She had no issues killing those who hurt people. She became a villain because she sought being in control. In power. She destroyed lands, villages, cities, and entire civilizations in gaining that land and power.

And in the end she became the Queen of Evil.

And after thirty-five hundred years, she finally got other villains to start up VilCorp, and the last two hundred they have ruled the world.

But now they wanted to put in a specific poison in the water supply.

"It would kill every ordinary person in the world. Look, I am not an innocent. I am not a good person. And I have very few morals in this world. But, I cannot get behind killing that many innocents. I mean, if you look at what I have done, how many people really died in my schemes? Well, besides minions and other villains… A few heroes. But I left kids alone!" When Catriona did not respond. "Look, I know a few ways to bring them down. I just need help. But bringing down all the idiots, means destroying VilCorp. Which," Etain sighed, "will mean that VilCorp will be no more. And I need a bloody hero." She stopped and waited for a response.

Catriona looked at Etain, "what did you just say?" Like she just had not been paying attention for the last hour, while Etain explained how she ended up in her door step half dead. How she knew her actual identity was another mystery, but Catriona was not sure she could handle that answer. But she now knew this woman's name. And why she became the villain. And honestly, Catriona could not find it in her to blame this woman for how she turned out.

Etain sighed. This was tiring. "Look, I am uncertain about many things in the world, including what side I am on anymore. My life went from simple girl wanting to be in a poly marriage with a nice girl and boy, and find another boy down the road. To becoming the 'Queen of all that is Dark and Evil.' So, look, I am over four thousand years old and I do not know who I am anymore. I thought of changing to leave this evil behind. But it was never over. My mind would take me back to when my entire life changed. When my eyes changed from warm and loving brown to cold and killer blue. I do not know much in this life anymore. What I know for certain is this: One: Aziraphale and Crowley should be everybody's OTP, the Ineffable Husbands are perfect. Two: Gay, Straight, or Puppet, everybody will have their own version of Bert and Ernie. Three: There are way too many sexual overtones in Supernatural for Dean to be fully straight (especially with Castiel), Destiel for life. Four: I am a God, took that sound advice from Winston to heart. Though you can make a legit argument that I thought that before that outstanding movie. Five: The Blue Brothers should have crashed at least once to Chicago with sunglasses at night. Six: People are stupid, Beer is good, and God got drunk when she made humanity. And last, number Seven: You are a God Damned Superhero and I need your bloody help! So, be a superhero and help defeat the damn villains! You almost legit defeated me at times! I never wanted to hurt you! So, I never did. Please! I don't beg, but I am begging. Help me destroy my brain child, so that way the kids of the world will be safe."

Catriona looked at her and just blinked. "Arc…"

"You know who I really am. For once, I want to hear a living soul call me by my name. You have my story. You know my past, where nobody else does, please, Catriona."

"Etain, I understand how you became a villain. I do. It only takes that one moment, I guess. I mean, I have heard that."

"Nobody is born a villain, no matter what some heroes and people wanted to believe. Ask yourself what is a villain? Nobody is born a villain. Life changes them, life makes them that way. Sometimes, it is just the choices we make that seem for the greater good that turn around and bite them in the ass. I knew a few like that, I mean they show their true hero soul in the end and end up dying for the greater good. They did not last long, even as a villain. But in the end what makes a villain is one event. That is all it takes. One event. Rather, the event takes seconds, days, weeks, months, or years. It just takes one event to change the hero into the villain. Look at the story of Medusa, she was raped by Poseidon, because he felt he had a right to her body. So, Athena blessed, cursed, her with a head full of snakes that would turn men to stone to protect her from the brutality of man. But Medusa became the villain and not Poseidon who raped her. Look at the story of Lilith. They cast her as the villain, because she chose to leave and become the mother of demons. She refused to be anything but equal. Men use that story to make women subservient. But women should use it to show men they can walk away. That they are not their slaves. That women were not created to be to be raped and to be bred. But to be equal. But at the end of that story, it was one event. Adam tried to rape her, so she became the villain. My one event was the death of my sister. So, will you help me? Look, I get the irony, I am a villain who needs a hero."

Catriona looked at the woman, who swallowed her enormous pride to beg her for help. The queen villain was asking her to save the world. Will she answer the call? Could she? She had not battled evil for almost three hundred years when the villains stopped attacking and started to follow the Queen of Evil. She looked into those eyes. Here was the Queen of Evil who still had her faith in heroes, and she was asking a hero who had lost her faith. But she did realize something; Etain was right. Nothing ever really was over, and they had a lot of unfinished business. "I have conditions."

Etain snorted, "of course you do, you are a bloody hero."

"Look, Etain, you can't keep running from your past. You will get help. I ain't always right but I am sure of this, you need to talk to a therapist. You will see it my way after you hate me and them for a while. You have used your anger and hatred to hide your true feeling: grief. Your heart was broken, and it broke you."

"Of course it fucking broke me! My sister was raped to death! MY NINE-YEAR-OLD SISTER, HE RAPED MY PRECIOUS SISTER TO DEATH BECAUSE A CORRUPT MAN WANTED TO CONTROL HER POWER!" Etain turned and whispered the rest. "And because I exploded and killed my father and the leader, it got my future wife and husband killed. It got my mother killed. It got my whole village killed, because I could not let them tell the other villages what I had done."

"You can't keep running, Etain. We will work together to stop this evil. But when we are done, you will get help."

"Help? What do you mean by help? I am fine. Totally fine. Fucked up in the head, but fine."

"You will be going into therapy. And you will fully entertain those thoughts of losing your Queen of Evil title. You can't keep letting the anger, the bad, the evil in your life overrule and bury the good. That is my condition." Catriona held her breath the moment she asked the next question. "Do you accept?"

CHAPTER TWELVE
AGREEMENT

Etain sat there and looked at Catriona. Could she make this agreement? Could she let go of four thousand years of hate and hurt? "It won't be easy for me. I may fight you. I will always question if I am doing the right thing, if I am on the right path. Life may be ineffable, but it doesn't mean I won't question this fresh path. Perhaps even more than I questioned my original path of evil. I have been in prisons, but the toughest prison in the world to escape is my own mind. I know this won't be easy. So, I warn you now I won't cry on any shoulders, or any of that mushy stuff. But you are…" Etain swallowed the vile. "There is no way to escape this, there is no place left to hide, and I have to stop trying to run from a landslide, and just finally embrace the grief. I accept this condition. But I won't bloody be fixed right away."

"You don't have to be fixed, Etain. You have to heal. You are still only human. You broke, and instead of remembering you were human, and you could heal…" Catriona shrugged. "You are no different than any other being in the world. You can be broken. But, you can heal. That is what makes us human. You were fearful of being hurt again. That makes sense. Your world was horrifically destroyed. I could not imagine living in your time, where you for sure property to be sold. In my times, it just seemed like we women were property. You can heal. And best of all? Seems as you have all the time in the world once we win." Catriona stated as she stood up, letting any room for arguments. "Now, let's get you something to eat. You have been out for two days. And we have to plan. And finish hashing out the details of our agreement."

Etain just nodded. She did not know what to say anyway. She laid her truths out. And Catriona said it was okay she was broken, basically, saying it was okay she took time to heal. Something Etain had been burying deep down and avoiding… healing and dealing with her grief. She sat there in thought while Catriona went into her kitchen. How had this happened? She had those villains under her thumb. Had she said something wrong to give them this idea? Had they heard her darkest thoughts? She had been so careful to not let the mind-readers into her mind by creating an almost permanent electrical barrier around her. Or maybe sometimes things just fall apart, after all, she had watched empires fall when there was no logical reason for them to have fallen. Hell, some of those she had built and then helped tear down. She had fought wars. Walked through time, hiding the fact she walked on a tight rope between hero and villain, by playing the villain. She was there when civilizations fell to ruin. Most recently she had been there when farmers won their independence from a dick ruler. She had seen civilizations rise and fall. So, maybe it was not her fault. Maybe just things just fell apart. Circle of life and all that rot. But all that took a back burner to the woman who had just walked into her kitchen: Catriona.

Etain stood and walked into the kitchen. "Look, I may be a bit dramatic here, but I am an over thinker, but do you hate me?"

Catriona blinked as she turned from the fridge. "I don't hate you, Etain. I hated your actions as Doctor Arc. But I don't hate you, and knowing your story, I understand you better now. You just never got a chance to heal from a broken heart."

Etain made a face. "Let's just never mention this mushiness again." Before she could think of her actions, she blurted out another question that always played on her mind. "Hey, if I was a good guy, would I have been your type?"

"Type?"

"If I asked you on a date, would you have said yes?" Etain winced, "never mind."

Catriona knew she should take the out. "I would have. You… you could make me blush. I guess the term is demisexual. It is sometimes hard to make sure I know all the terms, they change all the time."

"Tell me about it! And the languages! All the time! I mean, I know change is good and all, but once I get used to one way of speaking, they change everything! I just tell people I like pretty. But… I guess the term is… I don't know demiromantic."

"You have had so many relationships. Why is that the question on your mind?" Catriona pulled ingredients out of the fridge to make a simple pasta dish.

"Those weren't relationships," Etain stated as she sat down at the island. "That was just sex. Sex is something else. Get drunk or high enough, give them pleasure, take your orgasm to release those chemicals in your brain to be happy for a bit, and then get what you wanted from them. Sex is just that sex. Rather you are chasing an orgasm or you are chasing riches and power."

"Drunk enough? High enough? Have you ever been sober?"

"Oh, not since I became Arc. Booze and drugs were a way to numb me." Etain shrugged. "I had one relationship. I was thirteen, about to be married. I was always a bit cold to the outside, as you know I can be an extremely bad person, but I was loving and caring and attentive. If I was in a relationship, even as a villain, I would be that way. Someone that got into my heart like that, yeah, that bit of light still there? All that good would be for them. I could be in a middle of exploding a volcano," she gave a knowing smirk, "and if they called me, needing something ,I would stop what I was doing for them."

"Oh, why didn't you have relationships?" Catriona frowned, it did not sound like Etain had a consensual experience with sex since she was thirteen. Being drugged or drunk, one could not truly consent. Catriona vowed when… if… they got to that point, Etain would be sober, not even a glass of wine.

"To trust means to have it broken. To love is to become heart broken. And taking that risk, until you, I never thought anybody was worth it. You made me think maybe it was, but you deserve a hero like you." Etain shrugged, and changed the subject. "So, what are you making?"

Catriona wanted to push, but let it drop. "Simple pasta dish."

"Always a good go too. I like cooking."

"I hate cooking. I love to bake, but hate cooking."

"Want me to cook?"

"You are still healing. Are you going to tell me everything is healed?" Catriona glared at her, daring her to lie.

"Fine. I will just sit here and watch."

"Good." Catriona went back to work, "you know, just because heroes were the losing side, does not mean we were the wrong side."

Etain snorted, "look, I won't ever be a good little hero. But I will try to be less… evil. Both sides saw to much black and white. Life is full of gray and we forgot that as villains and heroes. Even I did. Which lead to me about dying on your doorstep. All you are ever going to get from me is that I will be less evil."

Catriona chuckled, "don't expect a miracle, Etain. So, what is the plan? Get all the heroes together and fight evil?"

"There aren't any other heroes. They all died. There are only those like you hiding. Not on either side anymore. I don't know if they even have their powers anymore. I know a few villains like me. I made sure they were protected. Innocent and all." Etain shrugged, ignoring the knowing look, and praying to the Powers That Be she was not blushing.

"What about new beings of power, do you corrupt them all?"

"There hasn't been a being of genuine power born since VilCorp was started. All those born with a power, they are so minor that most aren't even registered, they might as well be ordinary. Most work for VilCorp but never know their powers."

"What?!"

"We lost sight of balance. I doubt most of VilCorp even have their powers any longer. And even the board never kept up with training. So, while they are weaker than me, or you, there are a lot of them. That and they drugged me. And they have trained minions that are trained to shoot to kill. When balance was destroyed, the Earth stopped blessing gifted with strong powers. I…" Etain turned away in shame. "I destroyed a gift from the Earth."

"Etain, Earth is more powerful than every living organism, I think Earth just wants balance. But back to the point…" She took a breath. "So, none are born with power? Why? I get the not training thing, even I flex my powers, but I haven't done any hero work. But why aren't they being born with powers like we were?"

"The loss of balance. I thought, I thought this was the way to gain power. The way to be perfect. The way never to be hurt again and to stop the deaths of all the innocents in all the battles of good and evil. But I was wrong. Destroying the balance of heroes and villains by taking control and allowing the heroes to die out, it stopped allowing the gene from being passed on strong and powerful. It is diluted. I don't know if we can bring it back. But, perhaps if balance is restored, they will be born again. Power corrupts you know. It did me. I turned a blind eye. If I had not turned that blind eye, I would have blown up my own company a century ago."

Catriona snorted, "people are selfish. How do you expect to find heroes?"

"They are out there. The people in power, corrupt as fuck. Yeah, but there are people when the system fails to support basic human rights… They step up and provide. They would become the heroes. They are out there. After all, there are many who hope to see kindness and not greed in this world. It is just that they are a minority that are being drowned out by all the evil and greed of the majority. You see it, the first Pride Parade, which was actually a riot. Oh, those women were amazing, true heroes, Marsha P. Johnson and Sylvia Rivera."

"You were there?"

"Of course I was! I am one of those that like pretty people, and they were all so pretty. And I loathe hatred. Don't hate someone for being born the way they are. Gender is a state of mind. And sex and love, as long as all is consensual, and legal, doesn't hurt kids… get your kicks anywhere you like, love is love. And in my time, there was no hate against Poly relationships. As long as a man had a concubine to have an heir, have all the male lovers one wanted. If women wanted orgasms back then, go to another woman. And if those women of color can kick start the rights movement for LGTBQ+ rights! There are heroes out there. Plain and simple."

"For the Queen of Evil, you for sure are optimistic."

"It is a deep, dark secret of mine. There is a light in my core. I am not stupid enough to not know that. I always had a weak spot for kids, even with all the evil I did. I have a weak spot for those not treated as they should be treated. Hell, I bought slaves when I moved here, just so they could live free on my land. As long as people thought I owned them, they were not harmed. We all bleed the same damn way. We all have a heart, we all have a soul. And we all have our weaknesses. Hate… hate is a useless emotion. Even in all my anger, my hate fueled anger, the people I killed all deserved it."

Catriona laughed, "your deep, dark secret is that you are human?"

Etain shrugged, "I have worked really hard to make people see me as unfeeling. Feeling things gets you hurt in the end. At least that is what I was taught at a very key pivotal point in my life."

"Sometimes you have to break, feel, cry, scream, love, just to remember you human, Arc."

"Maybe, but everything is easy come and easily taken. I won't let someone hurt me like that again. I won't survive."

"What if they make it okay to fly? What if they don't break you? Fear breaks you worse than heartache, Arc."

Etain smiled, sad as it may be, as a plate of pasta was put in front of her. "Got any expresso?" Time for a topic change.

"Sure, let me get you one."

"I will take seven shots with a splash of cream over ice?" She smiled and give a pretty pout.

"Holy shit, just do drugs."

"Eh, caffeine doesn't affect me too much, it is why so much, something with the Earth currents powering me. And do you remember when Coke had coke in it? I was wired for the whole time! I stick to coffee now."

Catriona rolled her eyes. She went to the coffeepot and put in espresso instead of coffee grounds. "Can I ask you a question?"

"I reserve the right to refuse to answer, but shoot."

"Why aren't you upset your brainchild will no longer be, if we are successful?"

Etain frowned and held up a finger when Catriona went to talk. "One minute, I am not sure if I know exactly how to explain it."

"Okay, when you are ready." Catriona went and poured the coffee and set it in front of Etain.

Etain took a sip and closed her eyes and took a deep breath. "So, everything ends. I am no fool. I knew going in that it would one day end. VilCorp lasted longer than other corporations. Hell, I basically invented the word. If I stop and allow myself to grieve, I will start overthinking things. To be honest, that just ends up with me drinking. I was never really this type, you know the corporate Ice Queen, but I wore the mask of an evil queen so long, I forgot where I started and the mask started." Etain held up her hand and continued. "It is why I never stayed to wake up with a lover. Even when I had steady lovers, I was a wake and starting my day before they woke. If someone saw me in the clear light of dawn, I risked them seeing me for who I really am in this life. By allowing people to see me in light of a setting sun, they would only see my mask. You have seen me broken, Catriona. It has been well over three thousand years since I have been close to death, like I was this time. I am afraid to even show you all. I have everybody fooled with this mask. What is left of that light in my soul? It is surrounded by nothing but darkness and hate. So, I feel no true emotion about VilCorp. It was all about power, and protecting myself. Power was my armor. My armor has failed, and now I have to find another way to take care of myself. That is why I am not torn up. Because in the end, honestly, I no longer had a plan. I relied only on caffeine and fear to get me through day by day."

"Were you ever tempted to have a relationship?"

"A rich person giving you things, that means nothing. The busy person who gives you their time means everything. The only being I ever truly gave my time to, when it would not benefit me, was you. I wanted to see you? I blew something up. I wanted to flirt with you? To make sure you were happy? I caused a volcano to erupt or an earthquake. Ninety percent of the time when I was fighting you, there was no benefit to me. I never got anything from it but to see you. Four thousand years ago my father broke the innocent, naive girl in me. I could never let anybody close enough to break the woman I became due to the damage to my mind."

Catriona looked into her cup of coffee. Hoping, beyond hope, it would give her some type of answers, hoping it held the secrets of the universe, at least her universe. "I never had to fight to live like you. They raised me as a hero. My father died before my birth. My mother knew of my power since I was two. She raised me to be the good guy. They encouraged me in my child games of finding magic sticks and walking sticks that became magical staffs. They encouraged me to be a sweet, angelic, good guy. I never lost people I loved besides my mother, and that was too old age. I don't have answers, all I can do is help you with this, and stand by your side as you keep fighting, as you make alternative choices that define who your truly are in this life."

Etain turned away and snorted, "enough of the mushy. I can only do so much. Bloody Chick Flick moments. I am not that type of woman."

Catriona laughed, "nah, you are the tough, show no emotions type. I have some Irish Tea Cake, want some?"

"Sure. I don't bake a lot, it is time-consuming. I enjoy cooking better, no math involved." Etain was glad that at least for now this hero dropped the heavy stuff.

"When you aren't a world dominating evil, what do you do for fun?"

"Four thousand years old, there isn't much I haven't done. I read mostly. It is calming. I even write every dozen or so decades, sometimes stay with small cult classics, other times I am a big name. What about you? Last sixty plus years in NoWhereville, Iowa, what have you been up to all this time?"

"Owned a bakery. People of the town don't really ask questions as I 'sell' it and change my look and name every decade or so. I got used to the quiet life."

"Lovers?" Etain smirked, "I know you said you are practically Ace."

"Ace?"

"Asexual. I just am wondering if you have ever had a lover."

"A few. I mean, I tried sex. But it never left me wanting more. I did it just to satisfy my partner. I never got people who jumped bed to bed."

"I was also the one that was crazy. Sex was a coping mechanism. I always put on the brave face, even when I was scared, I mean imagine four thousand years ago and a thirteen-year-old in that world, on her own? I fought for every breath I took after I killed all those who were responsible for my sister's death. Men would take, and I had not mastered my powers. I hid them for so long, so my father would not do to me what he ended up doing to my sister. When I got older, around sixteen, seventeen, I discovered sex was power. When I was eighteen, I started using it. You could get men and women and every gender in the world to give you want you wanted or needed, and all I had to do was open my legs. I am a whore. I am no fool. But I own that." She held up her hand, "not everybody is built the same. I can't name the number of people whose bed I warmed, who warmed my bed, but I will never, ever regret what I did to survive. What I do to stay sane. You may not get it, but that is you. As long as you don't shame me for my past, I don't care. I don't need sex. I want it. I can live without it. But if the option is on the table, why deny myself?"

"I wasn't judging, just stating I don't get it." At some point Catriona would bring up the drinking and drugs to have sex.

"Okay."

"You know it is okay to be afraid, right? To ask for help, right?"

"You never show weakness, it will be your undoing."

"No, it means you have humanity, and still have something to lose."

"Only thing I have left to lose is my own life. My soul has been forfeited to darkness since I was thirteen and killed the majority of three villages."

"Etain…"

"Look, I am unsteady. Just do not give up on me. I will prove to you I am serious about this. But after four thousand years of anger and hurt, that is going to be hard to let go. My soul has always been unsteady, ever since I never allowed the wounds to heal. I blamed my mother, even though I know she had no way to fight my father. My father, I killed for his hated, he did not fight me though when I went to kill him. Maybe a part of him really loved my sister and I. So, Cat, I am asking you to hold on to me, I am asking you to not give up on me. I am unsteady. And right now, you are the only person in my life."

Catriona gave a nod and then let things drop; she knew Etain did not do mushy. "Let's get some sleep. I put a tee on the guest bed. Your clothes are in the wash. And there is a bathroom right across the hall from the guest room.

"Good night, Cat." Etain stood and made her way to the bathroom.

Catriona knocked on the door half hour later, "good night, Etain."

Etain did not answer. She stood in the guest room, just the tee on while her clothes were in the wash. She would go into town tomorrow and buy some more. There had been too much to think of today, and the last two days she had been in a healing sleep.

Catriona wanted her to go to therapy. She had even said Etain was her type if she stopped the evil. She looked at the moon, lost in thought. When this was all over, could she give her heart to Catriona? Her body was easy. She gave that too many, many people over the years. But, if she did this therapy and went on the straight and narrow path, she would want an actual relationship with Catriona.

And the people she had gone into business with now threatened that dream, that until recently had just been a daydream with no hopes of coming true. They really did not think about when they pushed Etain to the brink. They seem to have forgotten there was a reason she became the Queen of Evil. And they would pay for what they did, and would get a reminder right before the light of their life left their life just how powerful she was in this life.

But when the dust settled, could she give what was left of her heart to Catriona? She would not ask Catriona for her affections if Etain herself could not give her heart to the woman who has been on her mind for over a thousand years.

She bit her lip. She trusted Catriona with her life. But could she trust her with her heart? She guessed only time and… therapy, she could not even think the word without distaste, would tell.

Etain had always been one to be trapped in her mind since she closed down her emotions. The ability to feel had been long forgotten. Her soul surrounded by darkness, that darkness protecting the spark of light that was the girl she was once upon a time. Now she was asking Catriona to tether her to the living. What right did she have to ask of someone she had tormented for five hundred years?

The last couple of days with Catriona, she could almost forget that she made her name by being evil. She could almost forget that she had no right to ask anything of Catriona. She was asking Catriona to not only save the world, but to save her. She was asking Catriona to pull her out of her own darkness and bring that light back into being.

Catriona should let her burn. Etain was asking someone who knew all her secrets to tether to a new life. Did she belong in the real world? Would a therapist think she was too far gone? Her dark thoughts, her dark soul, the shit she had done? Or could Catriona really be honest in her desire to help her, to tether her, to steady her, to be there for her as she worked through four thousand years of mental problems?

Etain knew for a long time she had been spinning out of control. And now everything came to a head. And if she had not had plans for betrayal, she would have finally died, and left Catriona in a world where she would be nothing more than a plaything for evil. She felt the sparks before she saw them. Just the thought of one of them thinking about touching Catriona made her blood boil. She took a breath, and the sparks disappeared. It would not be good to let her anger get the better of her.

She sighed and went and laid down. Things would look different in the cold, harsh light of dawn. No need to put the cart before the horse. Catriona may want Etain out of her life after they won this war.

When Etain closed her eyes, it was a simple life with Catriona that she saw in her dreams, and that ache in her chest demanded she do all she could to make it a reality.

CHAPTER THIRTEEN
THE PLAN

The next morning, Etain was up before Catriona. She went into the kitchen, clicked on the radio she found, smiling wide when Queen came on, and found what she needed to make: pancakes, eggs, toast, and blueberry muffins. She made a quick rough batter for the muffins first and then moved to make the rest of breakfast.

Catriona walked into the kitchen with a yawn. She stopped dead in her tracks. There was Etain dancing in the kitchen to the radio as she made breakfast in one of Catriona's long tee shirts. She just continued to watch. And could not stop the unconscious prayer that she would get to see this every day for the rest of her existence.

Etain loved her mornings in front of a stove. She put on the music and started dancing. She did not hear Catriona walk in, and she went into a spin, using the spatula as her microphone. She stopped dead and blushed. "Umm… Good Morning."

Catriona thought the blush on her cheeks was the most gorgeous blush on this planet, past, present or future. "Good morning." Catriona stated with a smirk. "Is that breakfast for both of us?"

"Oh, yes. I thought we would eat before we started a base plan. And then go to my place and start calling those we know of that still exist."

"Well, it smells delicious. I did not think you would be one to cook, seeing you are a foul fiend."

Etain snorted, "I may be a foul fiend, but I have lived on this Earth for four thousand years and made more enemies than I can count. Plus, I was going to run my properties and home. Not, just go to work and come home to a sex slave. I would not have expected my wife or husband to cook all the time. Back when I was thirteen, I was trained as both an Heir and Woman, so, I would split chores with my spouses. As it was, our wife would have been the primary parent." She sat a full plate in front of Catriona and sat down with her own plate.

"Do you want a child?" Catriona had to ask the question. She did not, nor would she ever want, a child.

Etain chocked on her coffee. "What the hell type of question is that?"

"Just wondering."

"Do you?"

"If I had a partner to help, and they wanted a child. I just never found that person I would want to raise a child with, or willing to have one for in this life. I know I am not so balanced in my views. I was raised with some strict views and I only got out of being a vessel to give a man pleasure and give birth to heirs because I had powers. But if I had to answer honestly, no, and never have wanted a child."

Etain shrugged, "haven't thought about it since my future went up in smoke. I mean, I have been anal about watching my cycle and then birth control. The thing with my healing it also heals me to peak egg count too. I don't ever have to worry about menopause, unless I shut down my connection to the Earth. But I think that may just kill me. I never wanted more than an heir when I was thirteen. So, I can't honestly say one way or another. But, I am leaning towards, no. Especially, since I have no strong feelings towards a child, and if they didn't want one, I would still be happy with just them."

"Well, then you have plenty of time. You have a lot to work out in therapy, anyway. I have made a call to a local therapist that is knowledgeable about heroes and villains. He was born right before VilCorp took over. He just hides his powers and lives as much as normal life as possible."

"Oh, close to him?" Etain hoped it came out smooth and not like she was jealous.

"His husband is a friend. He has a minor healing power, so he is as long lived as most of us. Though most of us get our longevity from the fact, the Earth powers our powers. His husband is a former Villain. One that did not want to join you."

"Oh, well, there wasn't that many. Those that did not join were more middle ground anyways."

"Yeah, he has his dark side, his words normally dripping with acid and sarcasm, and if he does not like you, you will know. He was a bitter man before he met his husband. Their names are William and Whalen. I am sure they will want to help too. I told them the basics."

"And what was their response?"

"Whalen, the former villain, laughed his head off. He said he would come just to see the big bad Queen of Evil swallowing her pride to ask for help."

Etain blushed, "I wasn't even that evil. There was so many more villains worse than me. I am not exactly sure how I got the title. I mean, yes, I killed with little mercy, but they were murders, abusers, never anybody innocent. A lot in the beginning were fathers who sold their daughters to be raped."

"I know that. I even noticed that back when we were battling. I think that is why I accepted your gifts."

Etain blushed, "so, I was thinking I would draw a base plan how to get in. And we can start with a basic plan."

Catriona let the subject slide for now. After all, she would have to at some point admit she knew they were courting gifts. "We can plan in the dinning room, large table there."

Three hours later, they were arguing already. "We can't hold back, Cat!" Etain yelled as they went over the plan.

"Just blowing up the building is not an option! Think of the innocents!"

"No innocents work for VilCorp. Trust me, I know." Etain hired half of them to kill, the other half she had in her bed.

Catriona closed her eyes as jealousy burned through her. "We will not kill more than the villains. Those others are neutrals."

"I didn't mean I know because I slept with them. I mean, yeah, I slept with a good number over the last few hundred years. But I am a sexual being. And until this, I was sure you would not be open to…" Etain waved her hand at her and around.

Catriona rolled her eyes. "I am not going to ignore a cry for help."

"Look, Cat, you heard my cry and you are answering it. You are a hero. When I was yelling for someone to help me calm my mind, I prayed it was you that answered. I could feel you. All the time. I could feel you. I knew where you were, I could feel when you were hurt. There was a reason after fighting you many other villains, and even heroes, died. I never imagined we could be more than flirting partners. That was all my attacks were when fighting you. A chance to flirt with you. I need you now. And I can't let you hold back. I can't lose you. Not now. Not ever. I don't need that power anymore, if it means I can have you. But holding back will get us both killed. We will have to storm that building. We will have to kill. And it is time to call all who want to help. I know there are others out there. We have to be careful in who we trust. VilCorp had corrupted most who were left. I mean, I even sent you an offer."

"And I sent you a message to go take a long walk off a short pier."

"Yes, well, you always did have morals."

"You almost brought me to my knees more than once with temptation. And I wasn't totally innocent. I did accept your courting gifts for a thousand years."

"I was always bound to fall. I was selfish and always hid my powers until that day. That day, evil called my name. It whispered to me, told me I could destroy those who broke me. Kill the man who sold my sister like a piece of meat. Kill the man who raped her to death. When that temptation is presented to you, you sink to your knees and give in. I gave my soul to that darkness. What is it they say? The devil called my name?"

"That is right. You were born well before Christianity. Yes, it is said the devil tempts, said he first tempted Eve with the apple."

"Well, that route was more tempting than the devil with that apple. I could not say no. I did not hold back then. I won't hold back now. It isn't just because I am against killing these innocent, ordinary people. They tried to kill me! This is mostly for revenge. And if you hold back, we will lose. I am going to go take a bath." Etain stood up and walked away. Anger filled her. Not only for the past, but for the present too.

Catriona sighed as she sat down. She had to apologize. She understood where Etain was coming from; they had taken her power. A power she had killed to gain so she would never be hurt again. She sat there for a moment. Her faith in Etain was stronger than it should be. She stood and walked to the bathroom. She opened the door and her breath was taken away. Etain had not turned on the light. She stood in all her glory in the moonlight. "Sorry!" Catriona yelled, and then shut the door. She leaned against the door. "Damn it. Damn it. Holy Fucking God. She is gorgeous."

Etain turned her head when the door opened. She was never ashamed of her body. She rolled her eyes as she got into the tub. "Instead of taking your Lord's name in vain, you can enter now." She called out.

Catriona blushed as she walked in. "I just wanted to talk to you. And apologize."

"Sit down." Etain waved a hand. When Catriona sat, she sighed. "I am not asking you to be a villain, Cat. I am asking you to fight on my side, to save this world. You don't think I am questioning myself? I am an over thinker, always trapped in my head. If I wanted you dead, you would have been taken down a thousand years ago."

"You are asking me to kill! Maybe even innocent people!"

"If they attack you, you kill them. You don't allow them to get back up to shoot you in the back. You have to shoot to kill in this war. This is what this is, a war. The biggest battle the world has seen in a long time. If we fail in this eleventh hour, the world is dead."

"Etain…"

"Let me talk. I used the bones of the innocent. I used the blood of the innocent. I used the souls of the innocent. All to build my ivory tower. And because of that, it will be knocked down. Look, I have lived a life of evil and darkness and I am paying for it."

"Etain…"

"Please let me finish this. You want my secrets, I will give them. I am not asking you to save my tarnished soul. I am not a good person, this you know with all the time wasted fighting me. I have been afraid to lose control. Caught up in my mind and plans. I have thought myself to death about coming to you, almost literally this time. I came though, to you. I know this is worth nothing, as my soul is dark, damaged, and useless, that even your devil would not make a deal for it. But, I swear on my soul, I won't betray you. Just help me and we can set right what I put on the wrong path. And you are right, just because the damage to my mind has scared over, it doesn't mean I am healed."

Catriona took a moment. "You need to fight, and honestly, so do I. I lost myself when the battles stopped. I like the quiet life, but you are right, I could, and still can, feel the imbalance. I won't fight you anymore about the battle plans."

"Thank you." Etain blushed, "how did you know I was giving you courting gifts?"

"It wasn't hard to guess. I mean, the illegal medication to save my mother for another twenty years just happens to show up with a healer after I let it slip my mother was dying? Or the loan for my bakery? Or the fact it was paid off just a month later by some mystery contest? Orders every week that let me live a very plush life? Things that I wanted but would never be able to afford throughout a thousand years just showing up because I 'won' them?"

"I created contests from my many minor companies, your name the only one in the drawing the first year, did a couple more years, random people. And, the fact is, you wanted babbles. I was in a position to give you babbles."

"I accepted them. And I will be by your side through your therapy, and when you are ready, we will go down that road."

"What, no sex the first date?"

"What type of woman do you think I am?"

"Alas, I was hoping for a slutty one."

"Who says I can't be with the right person?"

Etain blushed and thought of all the naughty things she would like to do with Catriona. "Cat, you should go before I show you some of the dirty things in my mind. I don't know if I can stop if you let me go down that road."

"I will leave you now. And you would. You have morals about rape."

Etain just nodded that yes, she would stop with just one indication Catriona wasn't ready. "Good night, Cat."

"Night, you foul fiend." Catriona left, leaving Etain to her thoughts.

The next morning, Etain had already got them a ride to the airport. They were going to Etain's place, after all, she had more resources there to run a war. The plane was a private jet. Etain still had expensive tastes. Always had, and always would, from being one of the richest as a child, to having nothing, to the richest again, Etain wanted the finest money could buy.

"A private jet?"

"I have expensive tastes and can afford them." She crossed her legs, which showed off her calves and the fact she had overnighted a pair of Louboutin stilettos, and a suit that cost more than Catriona's entire wardrobe. Which Etain had hinted more than once about fixing that issue.

"Just don't spend thousands of dollars on a pair of shoes for me." Catriona winced at the thought.

"My sweet hero, I may have agreed to a quiet life. Perhaps I will write novels once more in my free time, but I will always have my expensive tastes. I was spoiled my whole life as a child, then gained everything I could ever want on my own after I became Arc. And I shall spoil you, my sweet. After all, my novels may become movies or shows and we would have to be on the red carpet. I will be the envy of the world with you on my arm."

Catriona sighed, "I can't make you see reason with spoiling me?"

"Dear, now that you know I have been courting you for a thousand years, I don't plan on stopping just because you have agreed to a relationship after my therapist agrees I am ready."

"Fine. I am going to read for a bit. And you mentioned something about calls, and your businesses?"

"Oh, yes, I do have to let my other companies know I am alive and well. I cannot let my stock drop. It is how I make money now. Stock market, business ventures, a long way from a girl who would have owned a village and farmed the land."

"That girl is still there."

Etain smiled, "read your book, dear, I will be dreadfully boring the next couple hours." With that, Etain pulled open a laptop and pulled out a phone.

Catriona tried to read her book but was distracted by how in charge Etain was when she was in business mode. It was a contrast to when they were alone, and she blushed at the most innocent of Catriona's flirting. She would have never thought the Queen of Evil had a submissive side, but it seemed it came out around Catriona. They would have to talk about that when the time was right. They had a world to save, and Etain would start sessions with William when they arrived tomorrow.

When they got to her place, Etain showed Catriona around a bit, the guest rooms, the bedroom next to her own was for Catriona, the kitchen, etc, not an in-depth tour at that time, and then went to her office, asking for a bit of alone time. Catriona was going to start making calls to the ones she had kept in touch with during this rule of evil.

Etain sat at her desk and brought out her journal.

I don't know where to start. I was almost killed. And I went to HER, Catriona. She has me thinking I can have redemption. I don't want to get to heaven. My soul was born hell bound. The darkness I have been through forged me. What I do want is just enough forgiveness to spend what remains of this mortal life with Catriona. Even if it is never romantic. I would take friendship over nothing. I have written in these journals for four thousand years. And for the first time since my mind was broken, I think I am ready to face the darkness that I have used to justify my actions, and head towards the light.

There was a knock at the door. Etain closed her journal and started to put it away as she yelled, "come in."

Catriona saw Etain close a journal and put it away. "I just got off the phone with Anthony." At Etain's confused face, "Freedom?"

"Ah! The idiot who wears his under garments on the outside."

"Be nice. He agreed to help. He will be here tomorrow."

"Thanks. I will try to be…" She swallowed. "Nice." She stood then and went to leave the office. "I am going to start dinner."

Catriona walked into the kitchen to find Etain on the phone and in front of the stove. She moved and took a seat.

"Moon, please. I told you I wasn't a relationship person. And you are happily married now." Etain sighed, "look, you said no because you fell in love with a hero. I left you alone. But you and your hero need to dust off those powers and help us prevent the idiots that said yes to me from killing the majority of the world." Etain paused and waited for an answer. "I live in New York. There will be a car waiting for you." She made a face, "thank you."

Catriona could hear the laugh as Etain hung up the phone. "Moon?"

"On and off villain. She has powers dealing with the moon, water tides, insanity, et cetera; she also has the moon phases tattooed on her forehead. She worships the moon I believe. I don't ask about that stuff. Religion and politics are tricky subjects. I talk about them with people, but I honestly am not one to be more than believing there is a creator, and She was drunk as hell when she made humanity."

Catriona chuckled, "I was raised in the early years of the Catholic Church. So, I celebrate things like Christmas, Lent, etcetera."

"Okay. That is you. Is that how you would have raised your kids?"

"With family traditions, yeah. I mean, they can choose what they believe in. But I know Christmas and stuff. So, yeah."

"You are going to want to do holiday parties." Etain moaned as she took the bread out of the oven.

Catriona chuckled, "well, yes."

"I am cooking. Your basic cooking will not do for a party. You can bake. But I am cooking."

Catriona chuckled, "I will concede, your food is much tastier than what I could come up with."

Etain nodded and finished the salmon, baked sweet potato, and a side salad with rolls. She served Catriona and grabbed her own plate before sitting down. She narrowed her eyes at Catriona. "Why do I feel like I have just been played?"

"I do not know what you are talking about, dear. You volunteered.
"

"I don't get how you can get me to agree to things. Do you have a secondary power to control people?"

"No, dear."

Etain eyed her, but went back to her dinner. Etain felt as Catriona was somehow 'training' her. "So, how many are we up to that will be invading my home?"

"I got four heroes, William, Whalen, Tony, and Ron."

"I got two villains, Moon, and her hero husband. And then I got Timothy, Pryo."

"What is Moon's actual name?"

"Oh, she legally changed it to Moon from Karen or something like it."

"Oh, who is her hero husband?"

"Some minor hero that has power over wind, his name is Bob or something like that."

"Okay, so we have seven, plus us is nine. And now we have these lists, you told me about. So, hopefully we can get more. How many are we going up against?"

"I made the council to contain fifteen of us. I had a majority, but I did want to make sure there was never an even split. So, fourteen, please about a hundred minions."

"Okay, so fourteen major players, hundred or more minions. We are at nine. So, almost even. How many names do we have on the list?"

"About thirty. But I haven't updated that in twenty years. Some could be dead, or dying. I know a lot of heroes and villains that said no, let their powers fade and closed themselves off to the source of their power, allowing them to age and die."

"Okay, after dinner we will make the calls."

"Yeah." Etain signed as she poked at her dinner. She may have been the bad guy, but so much was riding on this, and she did not know how it was going to work. She may be a genius, thousands of years old, and one of the strongest beings ever to be gifted with the powers from the Earth… but in the end she still was human; she could still make mistakes, and lose. Lose the world. Lose Catriona. Finally lose that spark of light her darkness has been protecting for over four thousand years.

"Hey, dear, this will work. Even if you are a foul fiend."

Etain chuckled, "if you say so, my sweet hero."

"I say so. Now eat, we have a lot to plan out." Catriona stated as she went back to her meal and small talk.

CHAPTER FOURTEEN
THE CALL TO ACTION

Finally, after dinner and a lot of small talk, which thankfully, Catriona let Etain let her get away with, she brought Catriona to her command center. "So, here, this tracks all the former heroes and villains that did not join VilCorp."

"You stalked everybody?"

"No, only you. I just kept an eye on everybody. Know your enemies and such rot."

"You stalked me?"

"Eh, kept an eye on you. How do you think I found you?"

"Didn't really want to ask too much. Or how you knew my name?"

"Okay, I stalked you. A bit creepy, I admit. And as for your name…" Etain bit her lip. "Volcano? Had my minions getting something? They were asking questions in your village."

"That is what you had them getting? YOU ALMOST BLEW UP A VOLCANO JUST TO LEARN MY NAME?"

"I wanted to know your name." Etain stated like it made all the sense in the world, and it was not in fact about the craziest thing that anybody ever did to find the name of their crush, okay, okay, Etain admitted, only to herself, that it was the craziest thing a person had done to find out the name of their crush.

"You seriously go about the courting thing the wrong way, Etain."

"Courting?" Etain stuttered. "Who said anything about courting? Just because I gave you courting gifts after that does not mean that was part of the courting!"

Catriona raised an eyebrow, "seriously, you did everything but actually just tell me. You let me win at times. You picked fights just to flirt. Your primary goal against me was to get me to blush. Even that battle was just to get my name. And we already discussed all the lovely courting gifts afterwards. So, it is not a stretch that you were already courting me. Probably since that first battle actually, now that I think about it."

Etain blushed, "oh, shut up." She pressed print on two lists. "You call the heroes. I will call the former villains."

Catriona smirked, "that blush does become you, dear."

Etain's blush became deeper, but ignored her and turned to her computer to start calling her part of the list.

After three days, they got a total of twenty, including Etain and Catriona, to agree to come and help. They were all coming to stay with Etain. Though they did not trust her, they did trust Catriona. And Catriona, the traitor, promised she would keep Etain in line.

As the heroes showed up and invaded her home, Etain stayed in her office or the kitchen. The first moment undergarment hero tried to start a fight with her. Of course she fought back. They had been trying to shoot energy at each other and trying to hit each other. Etain sneered at the 'hero'. "I was waving a white flag, offering you a spot in my home."

"You are a bad guy." Underwear boy yelled back at her, like it made total sense for him to be rude in HER home.

"I won't go down without a fight. But we are not here to fight each other. We have to fight VilCorp." Etain landed and crossed her arms. "I am not the enemy today."

"Why are you fighting against your own company?"

"Short story; they tried to kill me. I had to play dead to escape. I had backup plans if they ever decided to stage a hostel take over. They will die. I am not afraid to shed their blood. I won't give up. I won't let go of this fight. I will rather die than let them get away with what they want to do. I won't go down. I won't give up, until all of them and their minions are dead. I will let them know I am alive and paint a giant X on my chest. I have been through a lot of the worst the world has to offer women. But I am still standing. I am will save this world with or without you. So, what is your choice? Are you going to join me, Undergarment Boy?"

"My hero's name is Freedom. And I stand with the world. And hey, Phoenix is vouching for you." He landed on the ground and went over and held out his hand. "Truce."

"Truce." Etain looked like she would rather not shake his hand, but she took his hand and shook, giving him a little shock. She smirked, "sorry, I am the bad guy."

Freedom laughed, "let's get inside before Phoenix yells at us."

Etain nodded. She did not need Catriona yelling at her again. Seriously, give the woman an inch and she took a mile. Etain was still a bad guy! Bloody woman!

That was the start of the people invading her home. She, honestly, was not used to having so many people in her house. The twenty of them filled the dinning room. Etain enjoyed cooking for so many, but she did not like having to socialize. It left her uneasy. And that caused some accidental shocks to people who tried to touch her. Eventually, she just stayed away as much as possible. Especially when the undergarment on the outside of his pants guy tried to have a conversation with her.

"So, you a natural redhead, Arc?" Anthony asked as he looked around the home.

"I dye my hair with the blood of people who ask stupid questions when we are busy preparing for war."

Catriona came in to hear the answer. "Arc, please." She promised not to give her actual name to the heroes and villains invading her home. Catriona sighed as she showed people to the guest rooms.

Etain signed, "yes, I was born in what would now be the middle of NoWhere, Ireland during what is known as the Early Bronze Age."

"Coo, coo. So what changed you?"

"I don't kill kids. The villains I set up VilCorp with want to kill all ordinary people, including kids. I have few rules for myself. But one is you don't kill kids."

"Cool, dude. Need help cooking?"

"Can you cook, Freedom?"

"Call me Tony! I can chop."

"Fine. Follow me."

Catriona came by and smiled at Etain. "Thanks for playing nice."

Etain glared and went back to her cooking, tossing Tony things to chop for the stew she was making.

Tony chuckled and made a whipping sound as Catriona left the room. "Dude, you are so whipped."

Etain sighed, "she has another power. I swear. The moment she had my name, I suddenly give into her every desire."

Tony laughed, "that is love there, sweetheart."

Etain stopped and looked at him. "Love? I never said love."

"Sweetheart, you don't need to; I see how you look at her. So, what is your story anyways. I know villains aren't born."

"I was the eldest child of a chief land owner. The Clan Leader was the only one with more land and resources. I was to marry a boy and girl from the next village over to combine our lands. I was a female, but I was tough as any male warrior. As the oldest, and since my father never had a son, I was trained that way too. My mental health was always a bit fragile, like a Fabergé Egg. My father found that out when he broke my mind. When I was gone planning my wedding to my girlfriend and my best friend, the boy from the next village, my father sold my sister to the Clan Leader as a bride, as she let it known she had a minor wind power. My sister was nine. The Clan Leader raped her and my sister bled to death. They broke my mind. And I exploded with my power. I could not control it because I had hidden it for so long. In the end, both my loves, my mother, and three villages were killed. Historians blame a natural disaster, as the bodies stayed where they fell. In fact, my mother's body is in a museum in France. I have protected the place where I buried my sister, by owning the land. I swore nobody would break me again."

"Damn. I get you. Do you ever wish you could go back and change it?"

"Yeah. I wish I could be that carefree, innocent girl again. Things were so simple then, marry, have a blood heir, help my husband become a clan leader, marry another. We planned for two men and two women. I wish I had not grown up and lost my naïve outlook like I did that day. I wish I could lie in the fields of flowers, watch the clouds. Nobody has known my true name since that day."

"You can't hide forever, sweetheart. Now, I know you told Phoenix, but maybe tell William. Please, most of us see him for mental issues. None of us are exactly sane."

Etain thought about it. She flicked her eyes around. Could she have a friend outside of her love? Did she take the risk? She swallowed and whispered, "Etain."

Tony smiled, "Nice to meet you, Etain, think I am going to call ya Red though. After all, can't let that blood that makes your hair shine go unacknowledged." He grabbed another potato. "So, do you like sports."

And for the rest of dinner preparation, the conversation stayed light.

Once all were there and seated for dinner, one Etain did not know spoke. "You know Arc, I thought more evil, dark castle, and less insanely large light and open mansion."

"I have castles. In fact, I built one on the land I bought from Jeanne de Clission. Then after I bought the land, I helped her get three ships and a loyal crew."

They all blinked at her, and the one that mentioned castles went, "huh?"

Etain sighed, "female pirate. Her love was killed. She wanted revenge. I backed her play is all."

"Who exactly is that?"

"Pirate from the 1300's, her husband killed, she went around with three ships painted black with red sails and cut off her enemy's heads with an ax."

Tony nodded his head. "Cool."

"Back to the castles. I have properties all over the world. Some dark, gloomy castles. Others like this place. This is more my aesthetic, to be honest."

"So, what is the weirdest way you gained a castle, Red?" Tony had the strangest questions he had asked a million while they were cooking. And worse, he was growing on her.

"During the French Revolution, well, one of them, I tried protecting a kid and his family.

They had gone into hiding after the king was beheaded. Fifty years later, he left me a castle in France. The note stated, 'For our guardian angel, who said she was a demon. We are proof you have a spark of kindness.'"

Catriona smiled, she had heard a lot of stories like that these last couple weeks. "Always end up showing the spark when the world can't see it, right?"

"There is no spark. I just know how to gain what I want and need. I play the long games."

"Sure you do, foul fiend." Catriona teased her.

"Dessert?" Etain stood up. She was so done being the center of attention.

Catriona followed her to the kitchen. "I am sorry for teasing so much. I have a lot to learn about this flirting thing."

"You were flirting with me?" Etain stood there in shock as she got out the puddings she made for dessert.

"If you couldn't tell, I am worse than I thought I was," Catriona pouted.

"No, I mean, I wasn't looking for it. And I am stressed. I have all these heroes around my house. And just a few villains. So, yeah, I am blaming stress."

"You are doing quite well. You haven't killed anybody yet." Catriona chuckled, to lighten the mood.

Etain snorted, "thanks. If we are measuring my success by murder, do I get to maim the annoying Undergarment boy?"

"Oh, Tony is growing on you. If he wasn't totally gay, I would be worried he was trying to get into your bed."

"He is so not my type."

Catriona laughed, "come on, let's get dessert served."

"I should have put sleeping medications in the desserts. Then I would get some quiet tonight. And get some entertainment."

"Oh, shush. They will sleep just find through the night and we can start the planning tomorrow. It took us two weeks to call and get these people to agree to help us."

"Well, it is your fault it took so long. You made me play nice. I was just going to threaten their lives if they did not help us."

Catriona rolled her eyes and carried out half the trays as Etain grabbed the other half. "Behave."

"I am behaving." Etain grumbled, how had she become so whipped in just two weeks. Catriona had to have another power. Something made her so whipped. She would have to figure this out. She is now talking to her like an equal, had given this hero her name, and now suddenly this hero has a power over her that cannot be explained. And worse, she was making…. friends…

CHAPTER FIFTEEN
THERAPY

Why had Etain agreed to therapy? That was the question she was asking herself as she sat in front of William. She did not know how to go about this; she did not know if she could tell him. Telling a vague story to Tony was different. It was novel when he did not judge her. A hand dropped on her shoulder and she shocked them. She blushed, "sorry. Silly me. I…"

"You don't like touch. That is okay. I will get your attention another way. You have the right to tell people not to touch you. Are you touch sensitive?"

"It tingles," Etain whispered. "It is unsettling, like goosebumps or an electrical shock. It is uncomfortable. Very few can touch me. And most of the time, even they can't. Only time I could ever shut it off was with enough alcohol, drugs, and sex."

"Okay, let's start there. Do you have a problem with drugs presently?"

"No. I haven't touched the stuff since they took coke out of Coke."

"Liquor?"

"When I go the clubs, I binge drink, get drunk enough to have sex. Have sex to shut down my mind for a bit. Other than that, wines with dinner."

"I noticed that. We had to make a trip for beer as you only have wines."

"I like a glass of wine."

"Could you go without it?"

"I can. I don't always open a bottle. In fact, most nights I did not. It is only me normally."

"So, it is just the binge drinking."

"I don't think that will be an issue for now. Cat… I mean, Phoenix, wants to try a relationship. And I won't mess that up."

"I know Catriona's name. I recommended her to another therapist a long time ago. There is like four for all the heroes and villains that weren't part of VilCorp. How did you manage mental health for VilCorp?"

"Only the council was long lived, and all of us never thought in million years to go to therapy. I agreed for Cat."

"Okay. See, this is just us talking. I will not tell anybody anything spoken about in here without your permission."

Etain bit her lip. "Etain. My actual name is Etain. Tony said I should at least tell you. And you can discuss broad strokes with Cat. I mean, any worries you may have, etc."

"Yes, I see you have been becoming friends with Tony and Gabriel."

"We are not friends. I just can tolerate them more than the other beings. They are less annoying, than the others. So, I may keep them for entertainment."

"Etain, we will have to work on how you talk about your friendships."

"I am a bad guy?" Etain shrugged and did not look apologetic.

"You ego stays out there. Your mask stays out there."

"Fine, look, I know they are becoming good friends, you suspect it, but there is no reason for Tony and Gabriel to know or suspect that."

William chuckled, "okay, Etain. It will be our secret. So, tell me a fear?"

"I was once told the only thing I need to fear is a man with nothing to lose. But what if you are that person? I have always feared I would become like my father, where I became the type to no longer feel, even if I buried my emotions, and could lose what few morals I have and kill an innocent or worse, a child. Or worse, become like my mother, where I never fought back. Where I roll over and not fight. My mother did not fight for my sister. She let her get raped and murdered. My father sold my sister like he would have an animal to go to slaughter!"

"Do you have things to lose, Etain?"

"My humanity. Cat."

"Okay, that is good. So, you aren't that person. You have things to lose."

"I have been brought to my knees. I was betrayed. I planned for that. But after this, what if I fall back into bad habits? I believe you only get a second chance once. That once in a lifetime, someone comes along and changes everything. I know my first loves, were just the naïve, innocent first loves of my young life. I would never have connected to the Earth had they lived and died a normal death. Now, I am getting this second chance after go thousand years… And I am scared. What if I blow this chance Cat is giving me?"

"Look, you are here. You are taking the first steps. It won't be easy. We will start simple. But I will end up pushing you. And as long as you are fighting, as long as you are healing, you have a fantastic chance of making it through the other side. You may cry. But tears aren't a weakness. They are a sign you have been strong way too long. You have been alone and strong for too long. But you aren't alone now."

"We might need to go to a room that neutralizes powers. I don't like being pushed."

"My office is like that. And right now, today, I am just getting to know some basics. When we are done saving the world, I want to see you two times a week. After a few months, one time a week, eventually the goal is to call and schedule as needed. But that will not be for a while."

Etain nodded, "okay. I won't say I won't want to give up. But I will keep coming, keep grinding down these walls I have created, no matter how much it hurts."

"Good! So, your choice today, tell me about the first time you discovered sex, as you said it allowed your thoughts to slow. Or you can tell me about your sister."

Etain thought about it. "I have an eidetic memory. I found out about sex at twelve. Most girls did back in the Early Bronze Age. Most married at ten or eleven. I had a girlfriend. But to be with her, we needed to marry a male. I and my girlfriend would have sex. My best friend caught us. He preferred males over females but was… bisexual?"

"That would be the modern term."

"I liked pretty. I still do. He was pretty. She was pretty. I invited him to join. He was the first male I was with. Being with both of them at the same time was amazing. I was submissive to them. I was dominate outside the bedroom. But inside, I was a bit submissive. I never was again. From thirteen to eighteen, any experience I had was not consenting. When it was, I was always the aggressor after I lost them. I was about eighteen when I found out I could gain power through sex." Etain took a drink of water. "I remembered this one Clan Leader, I wanted something he had, just some precious stones, and I thought about stealing them. But, I noticed he had a weakness for the fairer sex, many times just taking them. It was a long time before I figured the word was rape. We just called it forced coupling. So, I went to him one night, after I drank my weight in alcohol. I remember tying him up, I remember having sex with him. I took what I was after as he lay sleeping. He had passed out after he came. I knew his hair was a symbol of power, so I cut his hair and with it I took his throne. He had been challenged the next day and killed by another who wanted to be a leader. After that, I used my body to gain power. I felt sick about it for the first dozen or so times. But then I became numb to it. When I took a woman and pleased her and then had her please me, I could almost sleep without nightmares. With men, if I was rough with them, I could wear myself out enough to sleep without nightmares."

"You were never rough with women?"

"No. I never wanted to be with women. With men, it came a bit more naturally to ride them rough."

"But through it all, there was no emotions, no relationships?"

"No. Most were one-night stands. I had a few steady…" She bit her lip. "what do they call them now? Fuck buddies?"

"Yes, that is one term."

"I had a few, most famously John Lackland. I helped him kill his brother. He was a rapist, he would conquer and rape. John could barely get it up unless he was tied down. How he pleased his uptight wife, I do not know. I had her in my bed too, at one point. I wanted to see if I could remove the stick up her ass. But honestly, she was too uptight and after she came she fell asleep not caring about her partner."

"So, sex for you was to exhaust you, so you would not have nightmares."

"Yes. That is accurate. It became a tool like anything else to help me sleep. Help me gain power."

"And you were always under the influence of something, liquor, drugs, etc?"

"That would be accurate. It numbed me enough not to mind the touch. But to be honest, nightmares are worse."

"So, I am going to tell you this now. No sex, for at least six months. I wouldn't say you would be ready for a relationship for that long, anyway. And when you do go down that road, no liquor or drugs."

Etain nodded, "I wouldn't go out for a one-night stand now that I know I have a chance with Cat."

"Good. So, we had a good session. I am going to give you a prescription for a sleep medication, ever take one?"

"No, I would have had to go to a therapist, right? And the only doctor I go to is a dentist regularly. I do go get a pap every year and STD test every six months."

"Good. I will set you up with our steady doctor, too. They will do your yearly exams. And since I guess you kept switching dentists, we have a dentist too."

"Okay." Etain bit her lip. "This was good, you said?"

"The easiest we will have. I fully expect you to scream and break things before we get you relationship ready. But we will get you there."

"Okay." Etain looked at her watch. "I have to go cook dinner."

"Can't wait. Until next time, Etain."

Etain nodded and escaped to her kitchen.

Catriona watched her run to the kitchen with worry. She turned to William. "Will she be okay?"

"She has an uphill battle. But she will get there. My worry is how she has used sex as a way to sleep without nightmares."

"Yes, I noticed she had them."

"I do not believe she has had a truly consensual experience with sex since she was thirteen, and her first loves died. Every time since there were drugs and booze."

Catriona frowned, she knew this and vowed to speak with her one day, "touch sensitive?"

"Yes. And there is my worry. She told me I can tell you broad strokes, and this is the biggest thing that worries me."

Catriona nodded, "I will be here for her every step of the way. I just hope she does not fight the healing more than I assume she will."

"She never thought of therapy. So, I will try different methods, but the easiest is just to talk, it seems. She relaxed once we were talking."

"Okay, I won't ask too much, but just to make sure she is okay."

William smiled, "she will be just fine, it will just take time. Just so you know, no sex for her for at least six months, it will probably be more like a year."

Catriona nodded, "whatever is the best for her."

"Good, now I am going to go see what my husband is up to. He mentioned something about explosions."

Catriona nodded, "yeah, Whalen and a few of the villains figured blowing up the exits would be the best to trap the evil villains in the building."

"What is bothering you?"

"These people have tricked the world. In actual life they are just toxic, they blame women when they say no, they hate, they buy their way out of things, for as much of a bad guy Arc is, was, she had some morals. These guys do not have any. How could she work with them?"

"They feared her. No, look, it took five hundred years, a development of a drug, and all of them to go against her. And they still failed. She wrote that all off as bad guy behavior. If she saw their sexual harassment, she probably spoke with that fake dominance that she has shown the world for almost four thousand years."

"Well, once this is over, she won't have to do that." Catriona swore to protect her.

"You can't treat her like a damsel in distress all the time, Catriona. She will fight back at that. She has always had a mask of dominance to the world. Yes, when you have sex, she will be more submissive to you. It is her sexual personality. But, even if it is a mask, it has become so much a part of her psyche that it will not be easy for her to drop when she feels safe. If she has actually ever felt safe."

"You don't think she has ever felt safe?"

"Think about it, Catriona. She goes from having her world destroyed and becoming a villain in one act. She kept hurting people before they could hurt her. She says she isn't the villain that had good intentions, but honestly, the only ones she ever killed were pieces of shit."

Catriona nodded, "okay, well, I am going to go see if I can help with dinner."

"Let Tony, friendships outside of the romantic one she hopes to have with you, will help her far more than hinder her in her path towards being neutral."

Catriona nodded, "I guess it is back to the command center for me!"

William chuckled and took his leave. Hopefully, he was in time to stop his husband and his… co-workers… from blowing something up.

Etain was absently chopping up some basil for her tomato sauce. She was making lasagna for everybody. She heard her name being called, "oh, Tony, did you say something?"

"Yeah, I asked if you were okay." Tony was worried about his new friend.

"I had my first therapy session today. He said I could tell him about my sister or about when I first started having sex."

"Choose sex, did you?" Tony moved to the side and started boiling tomatoes and cutting onions.

"It made me think, Tony. I don't think I have honestly consented to sex since I was thirteen. I mean, at thirteen I should have been married and a mother in the time I was born. Since then I got drunk or was drugged out of my mind. Sex to gain power, or something I wanted, or just to exhaust me enough I did not have nightmares of the hells I went through before I became feared."

Tony looked at her, "I am going to hug you. No killing me." He then wrapped his arms around her. "I was the same. Sex shuts the body down. There is a reason some cultures call an orgasm 'the little death.' You will get better. It will take time. But you got your mythical Phoenix, and you have me. And all the other friends you are gaining."

"I do not have friends. I have useful contacts."

Tony laughed, "say it all you want, but I am your friend, Red. Gabriel, too. And you have almost won over Timothy and Whalen too. You are stuck with us, oh Queen of Evil."

Etain looked down her nose at him, "you are entertaining. I may just keep you as a minion."

Tony laughed and threw an onion chunk at her, which caused her to throw some flour she had brought out to make noodles at him. Soon, both of them were covered in flour and various chunks of food ordained their hair.

That is how Catriona found them when she came to ask how long it would be before dinner. She smiled and snapped a few pictures on her phone. Yes, Etain would heal. She would never be the typical hero, but she would lose the title Queen of Evil.

Her new family would make sure she was never known as the Queen of Evil again. Catriona swore it on her own power.

CHAPTER SIXTEEN
TRAINING AND BONDING

Catriona was watching as Etain worked herself to death. She was not a fool. She knew why she was pushing them. The enemy had minions by the hundreds; they had powers; they were the super villains that escaped even the heroes of yesteryear. But she had enough.

Catriona stopped Etain as she dismissed the others. She had to say something to Etain. Etain was training too hard. "Etain."

"I have to get better."

"No, you are great. You need to rest."

"I cannot settle."

"What do you need?"

"I don't…"

"Etain, what do you need right now?"

"My mind to stop racing."

"How?"

"I don't know," Etain whispered. She loathed to admit a weakness.

"Take a breath. What do you need?"

"Sleep… but, I can't."

Catriona pulled her to her room. "Take a bath, I will be right back."

Etain sighed, but she did take a quick bath and dressed in the tee she had worn since Catriona gave it to her. Catriona came back just as she sat on the bed. "Cat?"

Catriona had put on her own night clothes. "I will lie with you. Come, let's try to get some rest."

Etain was tense as Catriona pulled her into her arms. But she eventually relaxed as Catriona just held her and ran a hand through her hair.

Catriona sighed as she looked down at Etain. She had been training their ragtag team to block against mind readers, against the minor powers of the minions, against the powers of the major players, rather or not if they still had their powers, and most of all, how to fight against them all without losing themselves.

Catriona sat there wishing she had paid more attention to Etain's actions before VilCorp. Perhaps Catriona could have saved her then, before the world convinced Etain her soul was damned. Saved Etain all this pain and guilt that Catriona knew Etain was feeling. For a hero it seemed to Catriona she had failed her greatest challenge. But she vowed to never fail Etain again.

Catriona was going to lie down when Etain turned towards her. It caused the tee to ride up. And there upon her thigh was a tattoo. It was the name FEIDLIMID surrounded by bog-rosemary flowers. Catriona knew bog-rosemary grew all over Ireland, had since before man probably. Feidlimid, her knowledge of ancient languages was rusty, but she was sure the name meant ever good. It must have been her sister's name. Feidlimid had to have been the luckiest child in the world to have Etain's undying love.

Catriona could not help but wonder who got to know her sister's name. Who got to see the tattoo it upon her thigh? It was a modern tattoo. Though Catriona had caught glimpses of ancient ones upon her skin. Etain was heavily tattooed. But she kept herself covered all the time. Catriona did not have the time to study them all when she healed her. And even after with Etain in just the tee, she did not get a good look at them. In case they caught her staring.

Catriona wished she could explore Etain, discover tattoos, scars, or even birthmarks. But now was not the time. One day, when Etain was truly ready, then Catriona would explore to her heart's content. For Catriona was sure of only one thing, and that she was fully in love with this villain that trusted her so deeply to be asleep in her arms.

For a villain that trusted nobody, for her to trust Catriona was a heady feeling. Catriona could not hide from her feelings any longer. It would be a long time before they could date, be more than just friends, but Catriona had learned that a person cannot run from the ineffable.

How could Catriona even think about walking away after this is all over? Etain had come to her. Confessed the most hidden secrets in her mind. Etain is finally lifting the veil of the lies she had hidden under for thousands of year. How could she even try to walk away? The writing was right there on the wall. Catriona was made for Etain, just as Etain was made for her. And Catriona would be there to protect her, dry her tears, hold her when the past threatens to destroy her mind. There was no way to escape, no place to run, no place to hide. And Catriona did not want to. She wanted to be by Etain's side for the rest of existence.

But that would have to wait.

Etain needed to heal.

To understand it was okay to be human.

It was okay to be unsteady.

It was okay to ask for help.

It was okay to ask someone to hold them while they gained their footing on their new path.

Catriona was lucky she had a mom who would die for her.

Etain's mother had betrayed her. Had given up on her and her sister.

Etain's father had given into his sins, especially greed, and it was Etain and Feidlimid who paid the price.

Catriona knew Etain was tired of being alone.

She could sense Etain was still fighting when she felt like letting go.

She could sense Etain needed someone to hold her steady.

And Catriona would be that person.

And one day, one day, Catriona would claim Etain as her bride.

For now, Catriona laid down and turned and pulled Etain into her arms.

Tomorrow was a new day.

Tomorrow was one step towards a new world.

One step toward the future.

After a long day of training after Etain and Tony had showered, they began preparing dinner. It seems to have fallen on them these last few weeks to be the cooks of the house. Others did yard work, others did laundry, others fixed the stuff they broke in training, arguments, or just being clumsy. It was like they were a family. Something that had given Etain some nightmares these last few nights. But she had not told William or Catriona about them. How could she? She could barely admit to having them for the first time.

They were sitting at dinner, and Etain let the conversation roll over her. Then a hero asked the villains, former or not they were villains, a question. "So, bad guys," Audra, also known as Temptress, started "what is the worse thing you ever done?"

Etain winced as they asked about the worst thing. It had been a lovely dinner until that moment. Because she knew they would expect her to answer, the oldest being after her was born about 400 CE, and they always asked her about ancient times. Most of the villains were the same, did some kind of siege on a town for some babble they wanted at the time and things were destroyed, people were killed, etc. Nothing major in the grand scheme of things. Hers had made history.

When it had gone silent, they all looked to Etain. "What about you, Arc? Four thousand years old, what is your worst?" Tony asked as he sat back with his glass of wine.

"Mine was accidental, I was testing the range of my powers still, even after over two thousand years. They continue to grow. I just could not stop what I started."

"Well?" Tony looked at her. He did not know if he should push, but something told him it was something huge.

Etain sighed, she might as well tell them. Etain could see the ash falling like it was yesterday. "It was a dark day in history indeed..."

Etain had been growing in her powers. She could control earthquakes, could even control the weather to some extent. Being able to control the electrical currents was intoxicating, as everything was attached to the electrical currents of the Earth. And she wanted to try to cause a volcano to go off. Nothing major, just a bit of spitting rock and ash. She had spent the last three weeks in Pompeii. An amazing city. The people, wine, food, all quite above what most of the world had to offer. And as luck would have it, there was a volcano close by! The city far enough away. All they would get is some ash.

She had gone up to the top. She figured it would be like starting an earthquake. But as soon as she sent her first current down into the center, she knew she was wrong. She panicked and sent more currents, trying to stop it. Her eyes wide as it started to explode. She looked to the town, all those innocents. But she knew she would never get them all out. She practically flew to the town and tried to get them to leave. But they would not listen. There were only moments left. She grabbed an infant, and she took off.

She watched from the closest safe point as the community was destroyed. All because she could not control her powers once more. She looked at the infant. She moved to the next closest town. She left the child with a woman that had just lost her baby. Etain moved back towards Pompeii. For the first time in a long time, a tear came to her eyes. She had long ago locked away her emotions, but she never expected she would have the power to do that. She swore to get her powers under control. She would control them, not the other way around.

Etain clapped her hands. "So, that was the worst thing I ever did. I learned to control my powers. Never would I allow my powers to control me and make me feel that helpless again."

Tony blinked, "what happened to the kid, Red?"

"Grew up, became the baker in the town, took over for the man they knew as their father. Had a long line of descendants. One of which is quite famous today. What? Just because I am the bad guy doesn't mean I don't have a soul. I kept up with them. They are still over in Europe."

"Well, I think that is enough deep shit now." Tony stated, "let's have dessert!"

Etain rolled her eyes. Tony was like a big, excitable puppy dog. "Well, go serve it, you have legs, Anthony."

Tony laughed and jumped up and headed to the kitchen, having achieved his goal of breaking the somber mood. He came back with the pie. "So, name a famous person you know that we wouldn't know."

Etain bit her lip in thought. She wanted them to know she was not always a bad person. "Oh, I knew Agnodike. She was a midwife that pretended to be male so she could save babies and women during childbirth. I stood up to defend her when they wanted to kill her. She is the reason women could then practice medicine in Athens. Backward place at times. I mean, women had power, but they couldn't be educated? They prayed to a goddess of wisdom, but wanted their women to be uneducated? Seriously, humans are messed up more than any species ever to roam this Earth."

"No argument here, Red." Tony stated as he handed her a piece of apple pie.

"Don't any of you get any ideas I am good. I have literally drank from the skulls of my enemies before."

Gabriel rolled his eyes. "Sure, Red. How about telling us another story?"

"There are love letters written to me in history museums across the world. From some high reigning people. There are poems describing sex with me that are taught in classes across universities."

"Yeah, yeah, tell us something good, Red."

"What do you want, a story of revenge? I have a lot of them. I mean, revenge can be sweet. It has made the world go round since Cain and Abel. About how I gained revenge on those who tried to betray me? Revenge on those who took what they wanted from me with no care about my well being? Honestly, that would be boring. Though eye for eye has been making the world spin since day one. I mean, Lilith wanted to be equal, so they damned her to become the mother of demons. Eve wanted knowledge, so she ate an apple and was thrown from paradise. According to most of your beliefs. Honestly, we all have creation stories. No, not a story of revenge. Perhaps of lust? Greed? Pride? Wrath? Envy? Sloth? Gluttony?"

"Red, stop delaying and tell us a story."

Etain sighed, "I have been around a long time. I have danced with royalty. I have fought wars. I have seen the best and worst of humanity. I am trying to think of a carefree story. I don't want to tell a story of heartbreak. I don't want to tell you a story about how nobody heard me scream, a story that I hoped was a nightmare, and my screaming had to be internalized because there was nothing I could do to fix it. Rather, the event was my fault or just nature doing what nature does. I have thrown parties where the booze and drugs flowed freely. I organized orgies in Ancient Rome. I threw orgies in Ancient Greece. Just because I did all this bad, fell to all these sins doesn't mean I don't know how to love. How to care. I may hide it behind the stories of sex. I may hide it by the fact I attacked villages, destroyed towns, but I never went out with thoughts of killing an innocent. I have killed millions. But I have never purposely killed an innocent. You want stories of my life, for what? Entertainment? I fought because I had to, so I could live. I am not a perfect person. I am not a good person. I fucking can't even be considered a decent person. But it doesn't mean I don't question everything. I have literally sat for hours, days, weeks, months, years, at a time questioning every action I took. How disappointed my sister would be in me? But I could not stop. Why? I feared what would happen if I lost power. You want me to entertain you. I am not a walking side show." Etain stood up and walked out, slamming the door. She did not know what came over her. She was not like this. She did not care about telling stories of her life. But she felt raw. Exposed. And she panicked. So, she did what she does best, and she ran

CHAPTER SEVENTEEN
THE FIRST STEPS

Tony and Gabriel looked upset with themselves. They stood when Catriona went to get Etain. "Let us. We just pushed too much. And with her just starting therapy, we should not have pushed."

Catriona nodded and went to fill up her wineglass. "You better not set her back. She is just opening up to all of us. She has a long way to go. So, be careful."

Both men nodded and went after Etain.

Etain moved outside. She sighed as she sat down on the ground and laid back. She looked up at the stars. She remembered the stories she used to make up for her sister. Stories of god and the goddess. Stories of warriors and heroes. How the heroes must have been sent from the stars to protect humanity. She remembered how she told her sister that the villains were heroes that had been broken. And they just had to find their way back.

Was that her? Did she tell her sister about her life? Etain never wanted to be a hero. She never asked for these powers. She wanted to marry, become a Clan Leader, change the ways of her people, and have a few kids. That was all she ever wanted out of life back then, and for her sister to find a love like she had, and they both would have lived happily ever after. But the Norns had different plans for them. Her sister was murdered, and she had been broken.

Etain used to know exactly how she was going to take control of this life. She was going to gain power and never feel again. Never hurt again. Never… just never have her heart ripped out of her again. And now she does not know where her life is going. She used to go and get drunk or high and then sleep with someone when she started to feel this way. But now Catriona was here, in her house, and suddenly the deal she made to try to work through her issues seemed too much.

She moved over to a tree; she moved and typed in a code and a safe door opened. She looked at the contents. Various drugs from her time on Earth, from the natural, to the man made shit. She had tried it all in her life. And right now she just wants to shut down. She did not want to think. She did not want to feel. She reached in and grabbed a needle. She also grabbed a little baggie in it was heroin. She prepared it. She sat there with her arm tied, the needed posed in her vein. All she had to do was push the drugs into her vein, and she knew she would not have to think or feel for a few hours. She was about to push it when she heard two voices yell her name.

Tony and Gabriel were thinking that Etain may have left. Right after Etain had told Tony her name, she had confessed it to Gabriel as well. They finally saw her standing at the edge of a property with a safe in a tree. The moonlight hit her just right for them to see she was about to shoot something. "ETAIN!" They ran to her.

"What do you two want?" Etain asked as she turned towards them.

Tony moved and grabbed her hand and took the syringe from her hands. "What are you thinking?" He yelled, as he checked to see if she had actually shot any of the poison into her veins.

Gabriel, with a flick of his wrist, destroyed it all. "Etain, drugs are not the answer."

"I don't want to think! They are the only thing that works! I want my mind to slow down. Not to remember all the bad thought I am forced to bring up in therapy and then you all demanding stories of four thousand years of a living hell. My past is not over. It never really was over. Because I never dealt with it. And suddenly everything is flashing through my mind and I can't stop thinking about all the bad. I just want the thoughts to stop!"

Tony pulled her close and hugged her. Gabriel came and hugged her from behind. "You don't need the drugs. We are here. Cat is here. We aren't going anywhere. We are so sorry for pushing you. We just want to know more about you. I know you aren't ready for everybody to know your name. But we just want to know what you did before most of us were even born. All of us. I mean Cat, me, and Gabe here are the oldest and Gabe wins that by being born in eight hundred forty-five in this common era."

"The oldest villain we are fighting aren't much older than you all. Most were killed by either me or heroes or themselves. I just did not feel I deserved the rest of death. So, I stayed alive. I am so tired all the time. And then this happened, and I still fought against death. I could have died, I could have shut off my connection to the Earth. But something holds me here. I just don't know anymore. All I know is I don't want to feel anymore."

Gabriel kissed her head. "Come on, I got just the thing. Horror movies and junk food."

Tony laughed, "come on, we can't leave Gabe alone, he might get it in his head to start some type of prank."

Etain nodded and went with them. Within a half hour she was in her pajamas, sitting and cuddled with Tony and Gabriel, watching extremely bad horror movies and drinking sugary drinks.

It was not much, but it was a first step in the right direction. It was a good first true step in healing. She was trusting these two people to keep her safe from herself. She would rise up from this darkness. She would always have this darkness inside of her, but it would no longer control her. She could only just take one step at a time. And this was a good first step.

"I knew the author of the Kama Sutra, Vatsyayana Mallanaga. We had what was the closest thing to a functional friendship I have had since I was thirteen. He was a good person. He was always trying to learn, though. He studied under many people. His texts were about how to have a healthy relationship. It was never sexual with us. Though, I have tried all the positions in the texts with various lovers. Some of them are not worth the trouble of trying them. Some of them are actually quite pleasing. Though, I swear someone just used the Kama Sutra to make up Yoga poses. How the hell does Yoga help anybody?" Etain opened up as Gabriel was changing movies.

Tony and Gabriel laughed, but it was Tony who answered. "Gods, I don't know. I tried it once to pick up the yoga instructor. It was for sure not worth the trouble. He was a very selfish lover. We lasted three dates."

"Eh, never tried it myself." Gabriel plopped down, "must just be good for sex. Make a person limber." He wriggled his eyebrows.

Etain laughed, "I tried it. It was not very helpful in whatever it was supposed to do. I got more peace from going and spending an insane amount of money on shoes."

"You are always wearing heals. You must love your shoes."

"I own some of the most expensive shoes in the world. I have ones with rubies, sapphires, diamonds, coated in gold, I like my shoes. They are a mark of power. I have expensive tastes. The right pair of shoes shows the world you are capable of anything. They tell the world to come to you, for them to make you their goddess, or to make you their enemy. The right pair of shoes can help you rule the world."

"Women and their shoes. I swear, I see shoes like yours and I wince." Tony stated as he remembered the knee-high boots she wore when training them.

"Shoes were a sign of being well off in most societies. We had feet coverings, but they were generally only for Clan Leaders and his mistresses. So, when they became more and more available, I started needing them. And when the last few centuries they became a fashion statement, I knew I had to have them."

"Makes sense. Okay. How expensive is your most expensive pair of shoes?" Gabriel asked as he filled their glasses up.

"About fifteen million dollars."

Tony spat out his drink as he coughed out, "fifteen million dollars? For a pair of shoes?"

"There are rare diamonds on them. They look good on me too."

Gabriel just blinked. "Okay, let's get back to the movies. Because that is just insane. I never owned anything over a couple hundred thousand and that is my house."

"I like expensive things."

"Without a doubt." Tony sat back, "push play, Gabe."

They all settled back into the next movie. Etain had opened up, she was not trying to go and get drugs, and they could watch mind numbing movies until dawn.

William sat with Catriona. "Something on your mind, Cat?"

"Am I weak?"

"What do you mean?"

"I have long since let Etain get away with things. Even when we were fighting on a weekly basis. We both let the other of us win. I should have just fought her. She was a temptation I couldn't say no to. I knew from that first meeting she was not going to be good for me. I was weak. I could not stay away from her. I think I fell in love with her that first moment I met her. But I denied it for so long. Hate and Love." She snorted. "There is a thin line. Then she just comes at her darkest hour. She asks me to save the world with her, and I just give in so easily. I should have said no. I am just weak. I should have sent her on her way after she woke. I should have not agreed to be her partner. Just help when it comes to the last battle. But I look into her eyes and I fall for her over and over again. So, I give in so easily to what she wants, I should be strong enough to say no."

"There is nothing wrong with being weak for the person you love, Cat. I should have said no to my husband a million times over. But I did not. Love isn't logical. But at the same time the most logical of emotions. The soul's heart knows well before our minds do when we are in love. When we meet our other half. You know, it is said humanity was supposed to have two heads, four legs and arms, but the gods fearing their powers split them in half. And now humanity roams the world looking for their other half. You found your other half in Etain. She can balance that righteousness in your soul. You can be a bit judge-y, Cat. You see the world in black and white. And there is nothing wrong with that. But there are shades of grey and Etain, she helps you see those shades. She is making her first steps into a new life. Just walk by her side, and learn from your mistakes and recognize your own faults…" He clapped her back, "and everything will work out. Now I am going to bed. My husband is waiting for me. Get some sleep, Cat. Etain is fine with her friends."

"Good night." Catriona sat there, looking out at the stars for a bit longer. William was right. There was a lot that was changing. And she needed to take things one day at a time. One step at a time. She may be weak, but there was not anything wrong with that. It was okay to be weak for the one that loved her and the one she loved. There was a difference in this weakness, then the weakness of letting someone walk over her. This weakness was not really a weakness. It was the path forward towards a new life. A happy life.

CHAPTER EIGHTEEN
A VILLAIN MAKES FRIENDS?

William, ever the shrink, decided tonight was going to be a bonding night. Sort of like in the modern movies where high school students drink, tell stories, play games. But they were going to ask questions, do silly dares, things of that nature. Etain did not know what to think about it. William, in the last session, also suggested that since Etain knew all their actual names that she should give hers as well.

Though asking a question to know about Catriona's first love was tempting. Etain still did not know much about Catriona's love life besides, she had discovered she was more on the demisexual, asexual, spectrum over the years. It may just be worth it to give her name to these… friends. She could always threaten them later or even shock them and wipe their minds.

"You will not shock us and wipe our minds." William's voice brought her back to reality.

"I was not thinking that. I was thinking it was novel I might have friends." She then blushed, "okay, I might have been thinking that."

"This will be good for not only you, but for everybody. We have been training and focusing on the upcoming battle. We need this."

Etain sighed, "fine. Fine. Fine." She threw her hands up in the air. She went back into her office. She pulled her journal off the shelf. She looked at them. She had preserved most and put them in air-tight boxes. The early ones chiseled into rock. What the archaeologists of the world would not give to get their hands on this collection? It told her story. It told the truth. The truth. She had, for so long, denied the truth from her words, actions, but never her written word.

On the other side of the office her novels. Fiction in most cases. In some cases the truth told to the world but, were sold as fiction. But she knew the truth. She sat down between the shelves and opened her journal.

I am trapped. Between fiction and reality. Listening to Cat has got me thinking about if demons existed. She seems to think the spark of good in me, redeems me for all the bad I have done in this life of mine. I sold my soul for power a long time ago. That illusion told me I was holy, untouchable, a god of my own making. But now, I have been forced to my knees and am paying the price for my sins. And Dabnos will gain my soul when I finally die. That darkness of the otherworld owns me. Cat, she and the modern mortals call it Hell. I have been so focused on running that I forgot. Nobody, not even a self-made god can run from their past. I thought I had won against my father. But how can I truly have left my father and the past behind when I never dealt with it? Now, Cat is carrying me to the other side. She has convinced me I don't need to be... this Queen of Evil. But, in the end, she will leave me behind. Will I be able to survive that? Or worse, what if she doesn't and I drag her down to the depths of the Otherworld with me? How can I say I escaped the past and the hell my father put me through when I still use his name as my last name? Still, let the world see me as his possession? This therapy is opening wounds I long since learned to ignore. Sometimes I wish I could just sleep until these wounds scab back over and I can stop the voices from screaming in my head. But, if I did that, I would lose my second chance... And that... That just may kill the spark of light still in my soul.'

There was a knock on the office, and William stuck his head in. "The night begins! Let's go! PJs and fun!"

Seriously, that man was more excited than the teenage girls in modern picture shows. But Etain got up and locked up her office before changing into a pair of yoga pants and Catriona's tee.

Tony was already passing out sugary drinks. Etain shuddered. She hated what too much sugar did to her. So, she passed and went and grabbed a cup of tea. She discovered teas in Asia a long time ago. Before most countries did. She adored tea. She loved coffee more, but tea settled something in her soul. She also grabbed a candy cane. She loved these things. She loved to suck them into a pointed tip. They came out in mass in the early nineteen hundreds. But since the sixteen hundreds candy makers had made sweet candy sticks. The pointed tip would be perfect to poke people when they annoyed her. She smirked as she took the candy cane out of her mouth and looked at the pointed tip before poking Tony.

"Hey! Stop that!" Tony glared at her.

"No. It is fun."

"Will you grow up?"

"I am grown. Wanna see how grown?" Etain smirked, she would not sleep with him, but teasing was fun. Teasing is what friends did.

"You don't have the right parts for me."

Etain laughed. "Oh, and Gabby does?" She smirked as continued to fashion her sugary weapon.

"Hey! Don't bring me into this childish game!"

"Says a grown man who became an archaeologist because he lost his favorite babble when he was robbing graves before he became a big evil villain." Etain looked at him with a smirk. She then poked him with the candy cane.

Gabriel started and glared. "Only you would make a weapon out of a candy cane."

"Would you three please behave?" Catriona sighed, "seriously, Arc, stop causing pain. What did Tony and Gabe do?"

"He is Tony. Enough said. I mean, he wears his underwear outside his pants. And Gabby is a bad guy like me."

"Hey! That was the fashion for superheroes at the time! I would change my outfit now!" Tony yelled, as Gabe yelled, "retired bad guy!"

"Good, I won't be seen with you in that old outfit."

"Will you three stop acting like children and behave?"

"Yes, mom." They all sang song.

William cleared his throat, getting everybody's attention. "Okay! So, first Arc wants to say something. Then she will get to ask the first question."

Etain raised an eyebrow from where she was lounging against some pillows with Catriona next to her. "I am making an announcement saying that I am awesome? Powerful? Queen of Evil? Cute as hell? Which is where you all have said I came from?"

"Arc."

Etain rolled her eyes. "So, my shrink over there says to face my past, I must remember who I am, and by that, I mean allow that you all know my actual name. I am Etain, Daughter of Brien."

"O'Brien… You used that all the time." Tony laughed, "you hid your name in your fake name!"

"Eh, it was a way to keep up the lie I sprung from nothing. But by doing that, I realized I gave the man power. That I am nothing more than something owned by him. So, I am Etain. I have no last name. I belong to nobody."

The others nodded. Many had similar issues with the times they were born. "Okay, so, Etain, what is your first question?" Tony asked as he plopped down with a bottle of wine, filling Catriona's glass and his own, offering Etain some as well.

Etain shook her head at the offer. She tilted her head and then smirked. "Who was everybody's first love? I can answer first. I was in a polyamorous relationship. My wife to be was named Bridgid. My husband to be was named Drest. I had been having sex with Bridgid since I was twelve. About four months in, Drest caught us. We asked him to join. I adored being taken by both of them. I was planning the final steps of my marriage ceremony when my world was turned upside down. The opposing forces killed them." They did not get to know everything right now.

While Tony was talking about some guy, Catriona froze. Her first love? While Etain was sitting right there? Etain was opening up bit by bit, and it was great. But Catriona could not help but get jealous when she joked with the others. Catriona always worried that she would pick someone else to date when she got well. And now Catriona had to tell Etain the story of her first love? That may set Etain off. She may just go back in time to them. After all, her first love story did not end well.

"Earth to Cat?" Etain placed a hand upon her's. "You okay, Cat?"

"Just fine."

"It is your turn."

Catriona swallowed, "you must promise me something, Etain."

"Anything."

"I am serious."

"I am too. Anything you want. Anything." Etain was dead serious about that promise. If Catriona wanted the world to burn, she would light the flame. Catriona did not know how much power she held over Etain.

"You cannot lose control. You cannot let your powers go."

Etain frowned. Why would a first love story need that promise? "Okay…"

"Etain."

"Okay, I promise. I said anything."

"You can't travel time, can you?"

Etain snorted, "nobody can but the crazy man in a blue box."

"That is a television show."

"There is a reason whoever created us made sure none of us had the power to go back in time. We can be super fast, we can fly, but none of us can change the past. No matter how much we wish we could sometimes. Everything happens for a reason. You told me that. You told me that many times through the years."

Catriona nodded and sighed, "his name was Paul."

Catriona was twenty. She had just met the most wonderful being. He had a minor power, so he stayed and lived a normal life. He believed that women were equal. It was a radical thought during this time. He started to court her. He would come and visit and they would just talk. They talked about books. They talked about the new university, Oxford. They talked about education for both men and women. They talked languages. And he was so sweet. He stated he understood she had no desire for sex. He kept his touches light and friendly. A kiss to a cheek. A brush of lips. Catriona fell slowly in love. She found herself on his arm whenever they went out. Happy and content. Perhaps one day they could marry.

It all changed one night. Catriona had come back from a battle with Arc. And had just wanted to lie down and sleep. It was late when there was banging on her door. She opened the door to find Paul. "Paul?"

"You tease! I have been patient for the whole year. Now, you are going to put out."

Panic filled Catriona. He hit her and ripped at her clothes. But before he could complete his crime, a rage filled Catriona and she let loose her powers. There on the floor was a puddle of Paul. Catriona blinked before she bent over and threw up. She ran to the only place she ran safe, her mother's.

"So, my first love ended up being that man that almost stole what is only mine to give." Catriona finished her story and saw Etain standing up. "Etain…"

"I need a moment." Etain moved and went outside. She took a deep calming breath. Why did people have to be so evil? Honestly, for all the death and destruction she had caused, she never took a person's will away. The right to say yes or no. She took a deep breath, trying to keep her promise to Catriona. She turned when a twig snapped. "Catriona."

"Etain, are you okay?"

"Your question about time travel makes sense now. But I am fine. Are you?"

"Yes. I was able to work through it a long time ago, Etain. To me it is just a bad memory."

Etain nodded, "just so you know, if I could travel through time, I would have killed him the moment he knocked on your door."

"I know."

"Let's get back before they think we are either killing each other or having sex."

Catriona laughed, "is that what the bets are on?"

"If it makes you feel better, all but Timothy think we will have sex and never fight again. Timmy thinks we have a big knock out battle brewing first."

"And what do you think?"

Etain smirked, "I adore you, I can't deny that. But you will push while I am on this therapy path. And I push back."

Catriona nodded, "good. Push if you need to. It sets boundaries. Though, I got to ask something."

"Shoot."

"When you talked about ropes during that final battle?"

"Have you ever been tied up during sex?"

"No. It doesn't seem like something I would like."

"Would you like it if it were you tying me up?"

An image of a naked Etain laying on their bed, tied down by silken ropes flashed through her mind, and a blush came to her cheeks. "Umm…"

"I will take that as a, maybe. One day we can find out." Etain laughed as she left a flustered Catriona in the yard as she made her way back to the group.

Catriona took a deep breath. "That woman does it on purpose. I swear." She muttered as she made her way back.

They were seated and Catriona threw an arm around Etain as Tony smiled and asked his question. "Wildest party?"

Etain smirked, "a deadly sin party. Now this one I will love to answer. The year was 1920, the rise of probation and the illegal trade was booming!"

Etain ran the best speakeasy this side of the pond. She laughed as she planned her next big 'dinner' party. It was a way for her clients to come pick up their moonshine, drink, party, and have sex. It was what Americans called Halloween, and the theme was dress as a deadly sin. She looked in the mirror, the passionate blue dress clung to her every curve. She, of course, was none other than lust. She had a pair of fake wings with the same deep rich blue feathers, with some deep purple to represent pride thrown in upon her back. Upon her face was a deep purple mask, and upon her head was a set of horns styled from her blood red hair. She smirked, a fallen angel just fit her.

"I remember this party!" Timothy yelled, "I was invited myself. I was posing as a bodyguard for some rich jerk to steal some diamond!"

Etain laughed, "I am telling this story for a reason. It will give you weaknesses of each of the fourteen remaining supervillains." She laughed, "take notes! Fun and work!"

Etain knew what each of the council was dressing up as, after all, she choose this theme for a reason. A bit of a potion from a witch made sure each of them dress as the sin they embody the most. Which meant their greatest weakness exposed.

"You have a witch?" William asked, breaking the story.

"Will you let me tell the damn story? And no, she killed herself when her son was murdered. Now where was I? Yes, the potion."

Etain was no fool. Most would be some interpretation of pride, lust, and greed.

She watched them as they walked in, sipping on champagne, with her arm candy for the night in her lap.

Richard Harrison came in with his latest heir making machine. Etain really wished he could kill him, but all indications showed the woman was willing. Richard was one to love to have as many children as possible. Which is probably why he was dressed in a royal blue suit and his latest wife was dressed in nothing but slave chains and a loin cloth showing her pregnant stomach. One day she would find proof to cut off his dick.

James Wilson came in with a suit of dark, rich, purple. He had a man and woman hanging off of him. Pride. Etain snorted, of course, what other sin would that man embody. But what was interesting was the guard. Ah, it was a villain, well former! A thief turned body guard. Hired for the night, it seemed to protect a giant rock upon his slut's neck. Well… she would just have to steal that., before Timmy got to it!

"Did you have to steal that diamond? I had planned for years to steal that diamond!" Timothy yelled. He refused to say he was pouting.

"Shush! I am story telling here!"

"Go on." Timothy sighed as he finished his drink.

Jerome Holmes, greed. Brought money and liquors. Jerome was never one that was very complicated. But honestly, that man should not be allowed to wear yellow. It was not his color. Though the woman next to him was gorgeous in yellow. Etain smirked, and made her way towards them, while finishing her survey.

Harrita Albertson and Kenya Abanio came together, wrath red mixed with sloth sky blue. Now that was shocking a bit. Harrita loved to spend money, and to spend it she had to earn it someway, besides VilCorp. She spent to much for that to be the only source of income. Was Kenya her other source? Kenya and her anger was not shocking. That bitch had a temper and a half. Etain and Kenya had more than once got into a fight because Etain could not stop the smart-alec comments. Etain would get her to the point where Kenya would have been killed if not for the contract.

Robert Evanson, green. Now that was weird. Envy fueled the monster. Huh. Well, that made a bit of sense, when she would show up with all the newest stuff, talk about another property, another company, he would slip one of his safe houses. Just to brag. Fool. She did it to keep them from ever looking for her true home.

Edward Nash and Zane Gbeho came together. Not shocking, they were married and cared little about anything but power and food. Thus the orange suits they wore. They really had let themselves go, however, their money did open up some of the best damn restaurants in the world. So their gluttony was their weakness. As they made their way to the cakes, pies, and cookies that Etain had purchased from her little sweet hero, Etain wondered if she could poison them.

Aki Han, Chan Ming Zhang, Juan Martínez de Palategui, and Diego López de Olivares, all showed up in yellow. Not shocking. They were all former heroes that gave into greed, wanting more, needing more, and turned to the dark side. They had their finest clothes and jewelry on tonight. Pity some of it will go missing.

"How much did you steal that night?" Timothy had to ask as he poured another drink.

Etain shrugged. "I am a bad guy. And it pissed them off. The next board meeting they all slipped safe houses, weakness levels of their powers, and just how desperate they were to keep appearances. It was worth it. Now I have two more! Shush!"

Howard Yang and Juan de Palencia were both in sky blue. Those two made sense that Sloth would be their sin. They never wanted to do anything. They were the first to lose their powers. Hell, she was sure they both were together because neither one of them wanted to do the work to have a normal healthy relationship. Making them work out, or work on a form, now would probably push their hearts to much. And if they were forced to try to use their powers… Well, exploding hearts!

Etain had made her rounds, stolen the girl, had fun with the girl, dumped the girl. All in time to swipe the rock around a neck, and babbles from the others. But the most entertainment came that night from The Empress of Blues, Bessie Smith. Etain adored her music. She was powerful, independent, and a damn good woman. While Bessie sang, Etain met many others she called up for the party. Robert Johnson smelled of a deal made, not with the metaphoric devil, now this was a deal made desperation with someone that would destroy all in the name of greed. Jerome.

Etain made her way to Jerome. "What do you want Johnson for?"

"So, I own him."

"How much did you give him to get a label?"

"Few grand."

"I will give you ten for his contract."

"Deal."

Once everything was signed, she made sure Johnson had a meeting with the executive at a label she invested in, but that desperation that lead Johnson to this deal, though beneficial, would cause his death. He would not be able to live with making a deal with a company that even had rumors of being evil incarnate and owned by the devil himself.

"Okay, so at one point VilCorp had a very nasty reputation in the religious community." Etain shrugged, "sue me."

"The point of this story, Etain?" Gabe asked as he filled her tea.

"Sins are a weakness. It will give us a game plan. Anger. Greed. Temptations. Lust. It is all there if we play our cards right. Use the sin that they embody against them, and it will lead to their death in the final battle. A threat to make sure Richard can't have kids, he will do something rash, die. Howard and Juan will probably kill themselves trying to use their power. I told you a boring story about my thieving ways, so you know that each bad guy has a villain."

"And what is yours?" William asked, wanting to see if she would answer.

"Kids. I can't stand to see a kid hurt. I will risk it all for a kid." Etain answered as she sat back. "Now that work is out of the way, what does one do at a slumber party?"

The others laughed as they refreshed their drinks and got out board games.

Yes, a bunch of heroes and villains sat around playing board games. While many of them kept up with technology, many did not, born in different times. Hiding that they were never aging, never changing, it became easier to become isolated.

What none of them knew, was that a turning point in history happened tonight. But they would not know it for a few hundred more years, when balance was restored, and heroes and villains rose once more in this world.

CHAPTER NINETEEN
THE FIGHT

Etain had a hard session in therapy. It exhausted her. She wanted to sleep. She wanted to shut down. She just wanted to be alone. She moved and sat in her office and grabbed her journal.

'It was a tough session today. I finally had to talk about my sister. We had been talking about my past. My sex addiction. But today William wanted to dig deeper. Start to get to the root of things. Talking about Feidlimid hurt. I had not been there to protect her. That guilt was what drove me to hide in anger and pain. William opened a lot of old wounds, pushing me to talk more and more about Feidlimid. He made me first talk about all the bad. The abuse of our father. Then how I discovered what had happened to her. The details I had been forced to listen to. The Clan Leader had actually bragged about how he just raped her to death. Tore her apart because of how small she had been. She had been smaller than an average nine-year-old. She had been too small, and the Clan Leader had the nerve to boost about killing her. And then complaining he would 'never have a bitch that tight again'. It hurt. I had just made it to the circle to hand out the plates of food. I had been told my sister had been married off. But had not known about her death until that moment. And to hear how she had been killed... It finally broke something in me. I had stood in shock, the Clan Leader going into his home. Before I finally exploded at my father. After all the bad, he made me talk about all the good. Helping my mother teach Feidlimid how to walk. Playing with Feidlimid down by the river. Watching Feidlimid be happy and carefree. With all this I am feeling so exposed.'

Just then, there was a knock on the door. Etain put her journal away and went and opened the door. "Cat! How can I help?"

"Came to see if you wanted to talk about your session today."

"I am fine. No need to talk."

Catriona frowned, Etain had not talked to her more than in vague terms about her therapy. "You can trust me, Etain."

"I know. I just am not ready to talk."

"If you want more, you are going to have to open up to me!"

"I am not ready! Do not throw that in my face. Do not try to strong arm me into talking about something I am not ready to talk about."

"How can I help fix you if I don't know what is going on?"

"YOU DO NOT NEED TO FIX ME!" Etain yelled, letting out a mild shock.

Catriona acted on old instinct and slammed into Etain and going through the wall in the hall to the outside.

Etain was not one to sit back and just take this. Words were not working. Time to let out her powers. She moved and slammed her hands into the ground, using the electrical current to cause a mild earthquake. She did not want to destroy her home.

Catriona was pissed after being knocked on her feet. And went and ran towards her, punching her with all the force she had in her body.

That set off a fight. One they had not had for centuries. All of their friends came out and watched in awe as Arc battled Phoenix once more.

After an hour of trading punches, clothes ripped, slight burns, cuts and scraps, Etain had enough. She had to scream. She let out a scream and shocking Catriona enough to push her back.

"Damn it, Catriona, I don't need you to be my light! I have that inside me! I just need you to sit with me in the damn darkness sometimes! I am sorry I am not healing fast enough for you. If you don't want to wait, don't. I will get well with or without you. But you can't be my light. I have to be my own light. I just need someone willing to sit with me in the dark." Etain sobbed; as she landed on the ground. She gave up. She could not do this anymore.

Catriona landed and went to touch her. "Etain..."

Etain had to get away from her. She had to get away from everybody. She just had to be alone. "Don't touch me. I will be back." Etain moved and went to her room. She stood in the room and packed a suitcase and grabbed her coat. She was walking out when she was stopped by Tony. "I will be back in a few days."

"I don't think you should go alone there, Red."

After the first night, Tony called her Red because of their conversation about her hair. "I am just going to another place of mine. I will be back."

"Not alone, you aren't. Sorry, can't let friends in this emotional state travel alone."

Etain glared but sighed. "Pack for colder weather. I realize it is November in New York. But colder, Tony. I don't have time to go shopping for a warmer coat for you."

Tony went and grabbed a bag quickly. He did not have to worry about the cold, his body temp was way higher than normal. "Let's go, Red."

Etain threw the suitcase into her car. "Hold on!" She slammed her foot on the pedal and zoomed away from her home. Away from the fight with Catriona. Away. Just away for a bit of time.

They got to the airport, where she had her jet waiting. She sat back and sighed. She knew she would not settle until she was in her sanctuary. This was a place nobody, nobody knew about, until now. Tony would. She looked over at Tony. "Did I ever tell you about this time in Baiae where I got Julius Caesar to give me a villa there?"

Tony looked at her and lifted an eyebrow. "Baiae?"

"More sinful than any city in the world. Ever. I should know. Richest for the time too."

"What did you do to get Caesar to give you a villa there?"

Etain smirked, "the year was 46 BC..."

Etain was lounging, quite in the nude, with Cleopatra on the beach of Baiae. She had been here off and on since the creation of the city about sixty-five years ago. She adored it. The sin coming from this place. Honestly, she had quite a hand in making it a sinful place. She even had a few villas under unique identities. She liked hanging out with Cleopatra. Of course, Cleopatra was addicted to sex. For the most part Cleopatra was dominate in her sexual appetite, which is why Etain adored dominating her. Cleopatra had been having an affair with Caesar lately.

Etain thought it was the closest to love that Cleopatra would get in this life. There had been a lot of bad with the affair from

Alexandria to Rome. And Etain knew of the plans to go and live in Rome with Caesar, hoping the ruler would name their bastard son his heir. It would end in disaster. That she knew for sure. Caesar had made too many enemies in this world. She knew of the plan that Brutus was going to put into place. That group was still bitter about the loss of the civil war. Etain gave it just a couple years before someone killed the selfish ruler. Etain may or may not have given them the funds to try to kill him. Honestly, the man should not have ordered the burning of Alexandria's library. Etain loved that place.

Though Etain had to admit, for such an asshole, he did know how to use that tool between his legs.

Just then Caesar came up to the two women. "Well, what do we have here?"

Cleopatra started practically presenting herself to be mounted. "Just a couple of sunbathers."

Etain smirked and turned to her side. "We are bored. Thankfully, the owner here allowed us to use their property to sunbath. How I wish I had a place of my own here." She had several, but Caesar did not know that. And Etain had an eye on one of his properties.

Caesar lifted an eyebrow. "Let's go to one of my villas." He moved and helped them up. "Which would you like?"

"The one close to Venus." Etain answered; she wanted the villa near that temple.

"Of course, my dears." He placed a hand on each of their asses. Etain did not like the feel of him touching her, did not like the feel of anybody touching her. Not until she numbed herself a bit. Thankfully, she knew there were some 'medications' at his villa that would numb her.

They walked through the city nude, with Caesar fondling them. But honestly, that was not shocking. There were many orgies going on in the very streets. This place was all about sin. They allowed practically anything the people consented to be done to them. Most people here had had sex with each other. Sex was not taboo here. Sex had not been for some time. It went in cycles; it seems. From being something shameful to being free for all and anything goes.

Once they reached the villa, Etain went on about how much she adored this location, as they made it to the bed, stopping only to partake in mind numbing substances before allowing Caesar to take them to his bed.

Etain sat in the tub after Caesar and Cleopatra passed out from their activities. She practically got away with anything right now. They gifted her many things. Jewels. Gold. She whispered in the right ears. She knew of events all around the world. She turned when she heard Caesar.

"My dear, I have decided to give you this villa."

"Oh, it is too much, Julius."

"Oh, it is not. After all, you made sure Cleopatra came up to meet me herself. And the three of us have had some great times together. Consider it another gift. I have already signed all the legal paperwork."

"Oh, thank you. Come join me?" She wiggled a bit and watched him harden.

"I do not mind if I do!" He joined her in the tub, Cleopatra joining them after a couple of hours.

Tony stared in shock after the story ended. "So, you fucked him into giving you a villa in a very rich, sinful, part of the world?"

"Sex is a very useful tool in life. I used it to shut down my thoughts. I used it to exhaust myself. I used it to gain power. You use what you have. And I had my body. It just became easier to use sex than to find other methods as I gained more power."

Tony shook his head. "You have had a wild life. You should write a book of your stories and sell it as fiction. Perhaps as a time traveler or an immortal through the years."

"I may do that now I am retiring from evil." They both laughed and sat back and relaxed. They still had hours before they landed.

They landed in Barrow, Alaska. "Why here, Red?"

"It is pretty. Isolated. Come." They got into the waiting truck and Etain drove them to her location. When they got out, she smiled. "Look at the view over the water."

"It is a gorgeous sunset."

"It will set today and won't rise again until January twenty-third."

"What?"

"That is how far north we are. It is wonderful." She unlocked the door. "Let's get some dinner. I only have a couple days here before we head back." Already she was calming down. And in a couple of days should be able to face Catriona.

After just a couple of days, where Etain just relaxed. Where she got things straight in her own mind. She went and hunted down Tony, who seemed to enjoy ice fishing. "I think it is time we go back. We don't have a lot more time to prepare for that ultimate battle and we left them all without telling them when we would be back."

Tony nodded, "we can leave tomorrow."

While Etain was being watched by Tony, Gabriel, who had been getting close to Tony and Etain as well, moved to talk to Catriona. "Phoenix, can I speak with you for a moment?"

"What is up Veles?"

"You can't push Red. She will open up when she wants to open up. She has four thousand years of pain, anger, grief, and whatever other bullshit she has lived through, to work through. She was born in holy water, then dragged through the fires of hell. She is made of both. And if you aren't careful, the hellfire will burn you and the holy water will drown you. But if you do it right, the hellfire will warm you, and the holy water will sooth you. It is all based on how you treat her. And you are a weakness of hers. Don't fuck this up, feather brain. She is a good person who had a lot of shit done to her in this life. She expects a lot from you. She expects you to keep your word about not pushing. Why? She would do that and more for you. Fuck, you told us yourself she found an illegal cure for your mother's illness. She would burn the world for you. She is trying to be the hero for you. She will never be a hero, not like you or Tony. But she isn't the Queen of Evil she allowed people to think of her as for four thousand years. That fucking mask is finally coming off. Don't you dare be the one that makes it go back on."

Gabriel left at that moment, not giving Catriona a chance to respond. He left her with her thoughts.

"Oh, God, I fucked up. I did the one thing I told her I wouldn't do. How do I fix it?" She asked herself as she sank down onto the couch and stared out the window. She hoped Etain would forgive her.

CHAPTER TWENTY
HEALING

Gabriel was a trickster. No doubt. He adored playing pranks. But he dished out his own brand of justice. He had the ability of illusions. He was one of those anti-hero types. He was glad Etain was back. She, Tony, and he were like three peas in a pod. And he now had the perfect prank to play on them all.

The next morning, people started breaking out in song and dance. And others thought it was normal. All through training.

It was during the last choreographed song and dance that Etain noticed. She turned and narrowed her eyes. There were few with this talent. She grabbed Tony and stormed down the hall.

Gabriel was sitting and watching it all on the cameras. He had his cup of coffee and a donut. He started when the door slammed open. "Red! Tone!"

Etain glared, "why are we dancing and singing?"

Gabriel smirked, "all delightful stories need a musical!"

"This isn't television, Veles."

"Never did get why you named me that a thousand years ago."

"God of trickery, magic, illusions, etc. Thought it fit with your powers and looks. I mean, you are pretty mysterious, have a nice shaggy beard, and from that part of the world. Plus, your name is Gabriel. Messenger of God." She shrugged, "I thought it was good."

Gabriel laughed, "more than bloody good. I loved the fact a full-blown villain named me. I mean, what do they call my type nowadays? Anti-hero?"

"Yes, so mundane and boring. There should totally be a third name for villains like us. Well, I sorta joined you in the group. Catriona says I have to behave."

"The singing and dancing, Gabe?" Tony asked, seriously could he ever stay on topic?

Gabriel laughed, taking out a sucker and popping it in his mouth. "Thought it would be funny. And relax everybody. I mean, your reunion with Phoenix was, shall we say, a little anticlimactic?"

"I am not ready to hear her platitudes."

"So, join me?" Gabriel showed his army of televisions.

Etain and Tony looked at each other and shrugged, "why the hell not?" And took seats on either side of Gabriel.

Eventually, William and Catriona caught them. Made Gabriel shut down his powers on them. And then told them to not do it again. All three sighed and went into the kitchen to make dinner. It sure was fun while it lasted.

Gabriel, Tony, and Etain were sitting in their little escape room. Gabriel looked at Etain, "it is time you talk to Phoenix."

"I want to stay mad."

Tony sat back and let Gabriel take care of this. Tony gave his two cents when they were in Alaska.

"Look, Red, life is all about blood, sweat, and tears. Why? Because life, and thus love, means facing your biggest fucking fears. You got to face her. You said yourself, this whole Doctor Arc bullshit was, so you did not have to face your past. Your fears. Phoenix had good intentions."

"Yes, well, I know for a fact the road to Dubnos is paved with so called good intentions. Look at me. I killed millions because they were rapists, abusive, and just plain bad people. Good intentions. But still secured my place in Dubnos, or as you know it, Hell."

Gabriel sighed, "she loves you. She just pushed too much. You both knew that would happen. Talk to her."

"I will tomorrow."

"Talk to her tonight."

"She hurt me!"

"You hurt her too. You pushed her away. Yes, she should have stopped when you said stop, but you threw things in her face that you shouldn't have thrown."

Etain sighed, "fine. I will talk to you tomorrow." She stood up. She really had to learn how to face issues instead of running.

Etain moved and stood in front of Catriona's door. They had not talked when they returned.

Catriona opened the door, she was shocked to see Etain. She was sure she fucked up beyond repair when trying to force her to talk to her. "Etain."

"Can we talk?" Etain was worried she destroyed the progress she had been making with Catriona. After all, she refused to talk, and then she used her powers on her.

"Yes!" Catriona cleared her throat. "I mean, come on in."

Etain came in and went and stood, unsure of what to do now that she was here.

"Sit down, please. Where ever."

Etain sat down on the edge of the bed. She was stiff. She did not do apologizes. She was not good at them.

"I am sorry." Catriona started, she moved the chair over in front of the bed and sat down.

"Me too. I mean, unfuck you, or whatever."

Catriona laughed, it was a laugh of relief. "I am glad you are predictable in your apologizes. Just what I expected of you."

Etain shrugged, "I don't apologize much."

"Yeah, me neither." Catriona took a breath. "I am sorry. I see you fighting with yourself. It is like you are a warrior, your sword is shaking, you are exhausted, all from battling the demons within. And I want to help you. I want to be your hero. But you are stronger than I give you credit for, stronger than you even know. You are working through all this shit, four thousand years of burying the event that caused you to stray from your path. And I should not have pushed you. I should not have been a bitch and threatened the promise of a relationship. You have to go your speed. You have to be ready to talk to me. If I push you, I am no better than those who took what they wanted from you by force."

Etain cleared her throat to stop herself from tearing up. "We spent one whole session talking about your eyes. I did not want to tell you that."

"Why? My eyes are a dull brown, not like your white blue, like the lightning that lights up the skies during the darkest storms."

"Your eyes are anything but dull. I first described them as honey burgundy. Your eyes are made of the finest amber with the hold of a black hole, sucking everything into its depths as they give their souls to you. Amber is made of a material that can take over living beings and freeze them for eternity. Your eyes sucked me in, and you have kept my attention and what may remain of my light, for eternity. Your eyes are anything but dull."

Catriona blushed, "umm... Thank you. But I am sorry I pushed you."

"I am sorry I got so defensive. I just was not ready. I don't know when I am going to be ready. I will try and open a bit more. But I won't say I will be more open. I am talking about things I have spent four thousand years burying deep into the darkest part of my mind."

"I won't push anymore. I will wait. I won't threaten you with the future either. Those were the most untrue and empty words I have ever spoken. I would wait another thousand years for you to be ready."

Etain cleared her throat again. "I will leave you to get some sleep." Etain stood and went to the door. "See you at breakfast. Good night, sweet hero."

"Goodnight Etain."

Etain moved down the halls and outside. She went and climbed up a large tree she had at the edge of her property. It was a blood moon. It was causing the clouds to shine red as well. It was gorgeous. She adored nights like this. Something about them settled her. She sat back against the tree trunk and just looked up at the stars. Could she open up fully to Catriona? She just did not know. Honestly, this therapy was making her raw. She knew she had to keep fighting through it, and in the end it would be worth it. She looked down at her arms that she always kept covered. They held the worst of the scars, though barely noticeable. She healed well. But there were thin silverly scars. She had only told William about them. He had made her promise if she felt that need to go to him. But she did not want to admit that weakness. She took out the small dagger she always had on her person. She pressed the tip to her skin. She watched the blood drip down her arm until it fell upon the snow that was on the branch. The red contrasting to the whiteness of the snow. The red of it tainting the pureness of the snow.

Was that what Etain was doing to Catriona? Was her darkness and evil ways tainting the hero? Did she make a mistake in going to her? Should she leave after this is all done? Disappear? She did not realize she was still cutting until she looked down and saw nine straight tiny cuts across her arm. She winced. She moved and put some snow on the wounds and jumped down from the tree.

She thought she had made it into the house unseen, but two throats cleared and she spun around. "Underwear boy, Veles, how can I help?" She hid her arm behind her back.

Gabriel turned on the light and looked at the floor, seeing tiny red dots of blood. "Defensive already there, Red? We haven't even confronted you yet."

Etain sighed, "what do you know?"

Tony came over and grabbed her arm. "We just wanted to make sure you were okay after your talk with Cat. Did it not go well?" He pulled her to the bathroom and pulled out the first aid kit.

"It went well."

"Then why this?"

"I…"

"It is something you have done for a long time. I can see the scars."

Gabriel sighed when she did not answer. "We aren't judging. We just don't want you to hurt yourself."

"What if I am corrupting Cat? What if I was wrong with going to her? What if I taint her?"

Tony sighed, "Etain, you did what was best. You aren't tainting her. Nobody is perfect. Everybody is perfectly imperfect. She has her flaws. You have even pointed some out. She is human. You are human. Don't do this anymore. If you feel the need come to us. We can help you with your fears. Your guilt."

Etain sighed, "I will try. It is all I can do. I know I now have friends. I know this. Logically. But sometimes, I just feel like I have no one to talk to about the mess that is my mind. I hate showing weakness. I loathe it."

"We all do, honey. We just take things a day at a time. We all battle issues with our mental health. There is nothing more scary than having to battle your own mind. Your own demons. We have been around for a long time. We have seen the best and worst of humanity. I mean, hell, even the villains were all against Hitler and the Nazis. I know for sure I saw you storming camps and saving people, mostly children."

"You don't kill kids." Etain stated with certainty. "I may be the Queen of Evil, but Hitler and his brainwashed morons were products of darkness itself. And that is saying something with the fact I have lived four thousand years. Very few could match him, Leopold, Stalin…"

"That is a fact." Gabriel stated as he helped Tony finish up wrapping the wounds.

Tony looked at Etain. "Red, we all fight demons. You aren't alone. You remember that."

Etain sighed, "spark of kindness saves the world, right?"

"Not the world, just our world. Our family is our world. Being kind to each other saves each other. We all have darkness. We all have demons." Tony hugged her tight.

"How can you forgive me? Love me like family? How can you? Why give me love?"

"Because I know what it is like to feel unloved. And you have had enough of that in this life." Tony stated, still holding Etain close, letting the tears wet his shirt.

"You suck, making me cry." She cleared her throat. "I dislike you guys the least or whatever." Causing both guys to laugh and pull her close.

"Enough of the chick flick moments!" Gabriel clapped his hands. "Now come on, we are having a slumber party." He ignored both Tony's and Etain's raised eyebrows. "And tomorrow we will talk with William about some anti-depressants. It is not a weakness to have to take meds. Each day we will take our pills, have moments of self-care, and live to flip the world off another day." They pulled her to her room, where they pushed her to the bathroom and gave her some pajamas to change into. Once she was done in the bathroom and changed, they pulled her to Gabriel's room. Where they all plopped down on the bed of pillows and curled together with horror movies on the television and junk food. Etain in the middle.

Etain felt protected. Was this what it was like to have brothers in her life? If so, she liked it. She just hoped they all got through this war.

CHAPTER TWENTY-ONE
THE WAR BEGINS

Just because the war would be one battle, it did not mean it was not a war. Etain stood outside and breathed in the icy, wintry winds. The icy cold air cut in her lungs. They were going to lay siege to her tower. She knew exactly where everybody was going to be in that building. Because two hours before they showed up, she was going to unlock some of the locked offices and labs. Not all of them. Not the one that held the poison that would kill the world. No. That one she was going to blow up. It would be one of the first things destroyed in this war.

Etain stood and watched the horizon, not really seeing what was before her. Etain knew that this one moment did not change who she was, not really. She felt something warm drop upon her chest. She looked down at the white shirt she was wearing. Upon it was blood. She raised her hand. A bloody nose. Should have known it would happen. Anytime there were significant periods of stress, she got a bloody nose. And figuring out who she was behind her Villain mask and this war, she was about to start and end in one battle for sure counted as stress. She was still a bad person. She was still someone who put up the tough exterior. She was still the one which did all the things that people called sin.

Except recently she had not done that.

Her entire time with Catriona, she had not once left to find some 'stress relief.' She blinked when she thought of the last time she had sex. She really had not had sex since the night before that meeting? Holy Shit, just how besotted to Catriona was she?

She shook her head. Now was not the time to think about her sex life, or what she had going on with Catriona.

Etain did not know what would happen. And for once she was worried about leading this group of people into a war. Heavy is the head that wears the crown. It had never rung as true to her as it did today. She had worn a crown for so long and never cared. Never realized the true weight of the crown she wore. Never wanted to care. She had led and killed minions almost all her life. Now, now, the people she was leading into battle, into war, were her friends.

Her friends…

It was still a novel thought, to have people to lean on, to have people care for her, to have people KNOW her.

But she could no longer lay on the ground and wait for this day to come. It was time to stop running. It was time to face everything. She could not lie on the floor and cry. She could not run to drugs and liquor. She had to finally stop running and face what she had created. She would face it all and win. She would not let the people she helped put into power destroy this world. It made her ill to think about just how much of a hand she had in allowing true evil to exist in this world. But she has learned from her mistakes, and today she will fix them. Today she stopped running.

After all, this empire she had created was bound to fall. Evil had called her name while in the throes of grief. Evil gained entry with minor difficulty. But something always held her back from being as evil as many, even if she became the most feared. Honestly, everyone who rose was bound to fall at some point, and she was no different. The humans gave her some entertainment in her millenniums long life. She hid away her ability to love, claimed she could not feel. But look what happened. She had found herself on her knees begging as she finally fell. The higher the angel, the larger the fall. She wondered if the mortal's version of Lucifer felt the fall as hard as she did when he landed head first into a pit of sulphur.

She had felt her soul had fallen into that sulphur pit. She had not even seen the betrayal until it was too late. And it finally had almost cost her the life she refused to end herself. She had no choice but to lay everything on the line. Then she fell harder than she thought possible. If she thought the fall from grace had been the worst of her existence, then the fall for Catriona had been the best.

Once upon a time her sister had asked her to explain love to her. Etain told her love was not the chain that her mother's and father's had been. No, true love was freeing. True love was the only thing that could give you true happiness.

Sadly, her sister never got that chance.

And that is when Etain had fallen from grace.

She proved she was just like her ancestors that day.

Damned.

All the actions they took, even if some seemed for the right reasons, were nothing but a whole lot of bad. They were a clan that craved blood. They had a history seeped in blood and war. And Etain was no different when playing for her blood sins. And no different in that craving for battle.

For the majority of her life, all she left in her wake was mayhem, destruction, and death. She left a trail of bodies. She choose each action she took after she came down from the blind fury rage of her grief, carefully. Like if she was choosing the world's best wine to go with dinner.

Funny how standing here contemplating how her life would change. She could only think about the bad that lead to this day.

The actions she took.

She never had been a saint. But she allowed her soul to fall into the darkness of grief. She had allowed people into her heart and soul for them to be ripped away.

She had felt that metaphorical sulphur pour and burn her throat as she buried deep any emotion and kindness of her soul. There was no more light to her life. No more shine of her tainted soul. She fell into the darkness of grief and became yet another damned soul.

Then came Catriona.

If her first fall killed the shine of her soul, the second ripped away the walls that hide it.

And this time, Etain knew, she would die if Catriona destroyed Etain's gift of her bleeding heart and torn soul. For Etain gave them to her to hold, to heal, to keep, and to love. If Catriona wanted to, she could destroy them, and that… that may finally send Etain to whatever version of the damned afterlife awaited for her.

Two falls she had taken.

Very different from each other.

But they both lead to this moment.

And her being besotted with Catriona.

Etain shook her head. She had it bad. Her life would change today. One way or another, everything changed today.

Today she would pay the price for all her past mistakes. Failure for once was truly not an option. She killed many a minion for failing her. Thousands of years ago she dressed and surrounded herself with lies. And today she would strip all that away and come out a damaged version of the young girl who killed three villages in her grief. She paid in full the price of her mistakes that day so long ago. She knew if she lost her friends, new as they were, she would find herself finally in a damned afterlife. If she lost Catriona, she would become worse than the ones she was going to destroy. She would burn the world if she lost Catriona. And right now that was the only truth she knew.

Today she would leave her sanctuary and fight. For so long her sanctuary had been turning a blind eye. To claim ignorance. Ignorance is bliss, is that not what they say? But now her sanctuary had become not ignorance, but this group of people who knew her. They still cared for her. They saw her pain; they have seen how she had hurt people, been hurt. Some had even walked the same road as she had, but they found peace and acceptance. They found a true sanctuary to be themselves. No judgement, no hate, no pain, just family. And now they shared everything, they all changed, they all finally found the humanity they had lost as they went through motions of life.

Catriona came up and put a hand on Etain's back. "Etain?"

"I am scared. Scared I could lose my new family. I am sad that I built this evil. I lost my way and am just finding my way back. I hide behind this Queen of Evil mask. I hurt."

"You are doing right. We will all get through this darkness. I am here for you. I will stand by your side. I will follow you through the fires of hell and will fight this war by your side. We will find our way through this war. I can't say it may not break our hearts. We are all aware of the risk. We may come out of this needing to scream, to shout, to grieve. But we will come out of this. We will make it through the dark. You will see, you don't need to run anymore. We will make it through this."

Etain sighed and laid her head in the crook of Catriona's neck, letting her take the weight she was feeling for just a moment. Letting someone help her carry the weight of this heavy crown. Etain looked up at Catriona. "I am going to say something. I don't want you to say anything. Not now. Later. When we can act on it. But, I have to say something, okay?"

"Okay, say what you need."

"I have seen the darkest parts of my soul. I have hit rock bottom. I have now opened up my heart. You can love me or not. I love you. I want to make love to you. I love the way you love to lie in the sun. I love the fact you wince when I change from wine to whiskey neat. You know then I am having a terrible moment. You keep me safe and sound, though. You keep me grounded. You keep me out of my head. It has come to be it is you I want to run too when I am finding that darkness starting to over my mind. I figured I have already hit rock bottom. I have nothing to lose. I have nothing to fear by laying it all out before this war. I love how you can't function until you have a tea in the morning. My heart races when it sees you, and I look forward to that thrill. I lay there staring at the ceiling every night, thanking the gods you listened to me. That you were there to stop me from freaking out. I am not strong enough to fight the monsters of my soul. I am not strong enough to leave you. I am not strong enough. I am afraid of the fact I may lose you. If I had to, I would sell my soul to your devil for just one more morning to see you smile when I practically crawl into the kitchen for a coffee. You and my friends have made this cold hallow house a home. I may have found you to beg for your help, but you, Gabriel, Tony, you three, you found me as my humanity was giving its last breaths. I was dying. That last light in my soul. I wasn't strong enough to save it myself. I needed you. I need you. Because of you, I now have people that I can trust to catch me. I have people that will be there when I need them. Not just when they want something. I have people to help me when my demons threaten to drown me. You have saved me. You saved the villain of the story. Typical hero. You can't help but save people. And you saved the worst of them all. I can think of a thousand reasons why you shouldn't love me. A million reasons. But, Catriona, I love you. I love you. And I will until I no longer exist and my soul is either given back to the stars or they send it to the deepest, darkest hole of eternity. Don't say anything. Not now. But before this battle, I had to let you know. I love you, my sweet hero." With that, Etain turned and went back towards the house.

Catriona knew why she had done that. She wanted to go and say the words back to her. But she did not move. She let Etain do this. But after the battle, they would have a talk. And Catriona would explain she would be there, waiting for her until she was healed enough to have a relationship. And Catriona knew one day, hopefully in the not too distant future, Catriona would ask Etain to be her wife. She moved and went the other way. She had to gather a few other supplies before the final meeting. Then the war's only battle would start.

Just because the war had only one major battle, did not mean it was not a war.

Etain went to sit with Gabriel and Tony. Tony was an actual honest to gods hero through and through, while the others had faults, Tony was a normal nice guy who was too kind. Etain smirked, "we get to be heroes for a day, Gabe. Just one day, don't get any ideas there underwear boy!"

Tony laughed, "you two should never have been villains. Gabe was more of a trickster that played pranks, and you, well, the only actual people you killed were pieces of shit."

Gabriel raised an eyebrow as he looked up from his bomb. "We are horrible, no good villains. Don't you forget that, Tony."

Tony laughed, "come on, we need to get this all done. We got a war to win today."

Etain nodded, going quiet. But she swallowed the fear. They all knew the ask. She nodded again. "Let's finish up."

Etain stood in front of her friends, her new family. "We will make our stand today. We may fall. I won't lie to you. What happens here today won't ever make the history books. After all is said and done I will burn VilCorp to the ground. The company will not recover. These villains were some of the worst when we ran the world. They won't show mercy. You can't show mercy. Lady Mercy has no place in our lives tonight. We can't waste time playing. Fight, give it all. You all answered the call tonight. You did not have to come and fight this war. But you did. For that, I will be eternally grateful. I never expected any of you to come. I never expected to find a family in the most unlikely of places. Every day for the last four thousand years, a piece of me was dying. My body couldn't die, but my soul could decay. You have all had a part in healing that. I have toed the line of being a true villain and being what I was, The Queen of Evil was an illusion. But no matter what I did learn, karma catches up to you. I had to fall so I could rise. Karma did not care if I was rich, famous, only that it was time to pay for my actions. Today their karma will catch up to them. We will win. Their struggles will all be in vain. We have grown and we are powerful, our voices will be heard. We are fighting for the right to live today. For all the ordinary people to live. For the Earth to live. It is time to go. One last chance to back out before the hammer falls." There was silence. "Then everybody, today is the day. Today we lay siege to VilCorp and destroy what it took me one thousand years to build."

With that, they all stood. With that they all left the place that had become their home, their training center, their life, these last few months. Today they would fight for the humans they once had sworn to protect, or the ones they wished to one day dominate and learned better.

Today there were no heroes and villains. Today there was the enemy, fourteen enemies. And there was this ragtag team.

Today the Queen of Evil would destroy everything she built.

Today the Queen of Evil would fall.

Fall to the woman she had been protecting for the last four thousand years.

Today there was Etain.

Not Doctor Arc.

There were not villains.

There were not heroes.

Today there was only the enemy and those dumb enough to fight them.

Today, losing was not an option.

There would not be another day to fight if they lost today.

For all would be lost, if they lost.

CHAPTER TWENTY-TWO
FINAL BATTLE

They laid siege to the tower. They all even put on their old outfits for this war. Well, Etain made Tony update his, no underwear over his clothes. They were not hiding the fact they had powers. Let the world know the old myths were true. And it was time for the villains to fall once more.

Doctor Arc stood in front of the building. Her eyes shined with power as her hair whipped around her. She smirked as she looked at the others.

It was time for a show.

For they stood by her.

She would be damned again before she did not stand for them.

She came from a living hell.

She created a wall against the world.

And now it was time to tear it down.

The teams were all on the roof, waiting for the signal. Except for three.

Etain walked in Tony and Gabriel flanking her right and left sides, the receptionist started whispering.

After all, Etain was 'missing.'

Etain got rid of the company.

So, they whispered.

Which is what she wanted, after all, the bad guys had to know they were there.

Etain ignored them and lead Tony and Gabriel down to the labs. They had maintenance uniforms over their outfits. Etain looked at them as they stopped at the door. "The signal for the others, is the blast. The signal for you, is when I press this button and your vest lights up. I am going to go and 'speak' with James." She gave an evil smirk. Speaking would be the last thing on her mind.

"Be careful, Red. We just gained our sister, and we don't need to be losing you before we can wreak havoc among the world."

Etain gave them a smile. The song Silent Night played through the speakers, Christmas music. She forgot Christmas was next week. Well, the world was getting a Christmas gift. "You two… don't die. I can't train more 'friends.'"

Both laughed and wrapped her up in a bear hug.

Etain nodded, and she walked away. She dropped the trench coat she had worn. She loved her body hugging Doctor Arc outfit. Even if it had not seen the light of day in five hundred years. There was just one difference in the black, rippled, shiny leather suit.

Catriona had added a Phoenix. Not the standard fire one, not even the Earth one that rested upon her outfit. No, this one was surrounded by the arcs of electricity, it was the color of her hair, with eyes that shined with the power of the currents of the Earth, with just enough of her original honey color underneath, to show the hero under the mask.

She had told Catriona about how her eyes changed. Catriona teased her about changing her blue eyes to brown once more, that her blue eyes were a mask protecting the light within Etain's soul.

Etain stopped in front of the office, her office. She walked in and smirked; she moved and sat down at her desk. She pressed a button, an announcement to the place. "All but the council shall leave the property immediately. As of now, per the decree of the owner of this land, VilCorp is now, and forever closed. See your unemployment center, severances will be in your bank in a week. Good bye. And enjoy your lives."

James had been basically raping his newest assistant when the voice came across the intercom. The bitch was alive. He moved quickly and hissed a warning to the assistant. "Don't fucking move. I will be back in a few." James ran out the door, zipping up his pants.

He made it up to her office and slammed the door open. "Bitch, how are you alive?"

Etain stood in her full glory. "My need for your death was larger than the will of death. Death will accept the fourteen of you in exchange for one dirty, tainted soul."

James snorted, "like there is a death that can make deals."

Etain shrugged as she walked around and leaned against the front of her desk. "I don't know. But I chose to hold a funeral for my masks. I chose to stop running. And I can't let you kill innocents. I turned a blind eye to the shit you and the others have done. But no more. Because, guess what I killed more people for a lot less than the shit that you have done." She pushed herself away from the desk and walked up to him, whispering in his ear. "Do you want me to list your sins? Do you want to repent, James?" She hissed his name and smirked at the shiver of fear.

James swallowed, he turned and ran. Under it all, he was a greedy coward. And she had to have more power in her than they thought if she was alive. He moved, she had a weakness. They all knew that hero was a weakness when Etain refused to kill her or allow another villain to kill her when they were having battles on a weekly basis back in the good ole days. That hero. He could see if the being was alive. But he was blasted into a wall from what felt like an earthquake.

When James ran, she pressed the button. The computer system having notified her that all but the council and one person were in the building. The person would be evacuated by one of the others. She braced herself for the blast. She then strutted out of the office. "The war begins and ends today, James."

James felt his head feeling the blood. "Who is here with you?"

"The heroes that are heroes." She moved and used a current to knock him out. "I will come back for you. I want you to see it all end. I want you to watch the end." She walked away. She had two others to destroy. Richard and Jerome. They were the heads of the hydra that betrayed her. Except this time, the heads would not have a chance to grow back. She moved back to her office.

"Esteemed council members! The fourteen of you, have figured out who I am. You have also discovered you are unable to leave. Today is the day you all finally die. Go to whatever evil afterlife you believe in. Because you pushed me to a brink. And you forgot just how I got the title Queen of Evil. It is because I have no soul!" She smirked as she kept her finger on the button. "And now, you get to all see me in all my glory." She walked out of the office. First stop: Jerome.

Jerome was trying to get out of his window when Etain made her way into the room. He turned and swallowed. "Now Arc, if I didn't go along with it, James would have had me killed like he had you killed." He swallowed when he heard two screams, and shuddered as they were suddenly cut off.

"I am going to guess that was Howard Yang and Juan de Palencia. Probably tried to use their powers and they exploded, we both know they were the first to lose their powers. What about your Jerome, do you still have your powers? I mean we both know you had air powers. Do you think you can still fly?" She smirked as she knelt down and let the currents run through the floor, not to kill him outright. But the currents did throw him into his office window, the bulletproof glass, cracked. Jerome tried to stand. "Arc…"

"I am not here to show mercy. I am not here to give you a chance to fight. I am here to destroy everything." Etain threw the current and it threw him through the window. "Can you fly, Mohandas?" She tilted her head as she watched him try to use his powers, but in the end he slammed into the ground below the building. Blood was everywhere. She jumped and flew down to check. She used the currents to remove his head.

Etain saw Tony and Gabe as they fought with Aki Han, Chan Ming Zhang, Juan Martínez de Palategui, and Diego López de Olivares. She moved to join them when Gabe shook his head.

Tony smirked, "Freedom and Veles, will win against all you greedy, weak powered villains!" He screamed as he picked up a part of the building and used it as a baseball bat, while Veles used an illusion to appear in a dozen different spots to cause the villains to stand back to back in a circle.

Veles smirked as the beam hit the villains and they went flying.

Etain nodded to them and left to check Catriona.

Catriona was fighting Harrita Albertson and Kenya Abanio. Catriona had just sent a blast of her power to Harrita, and she exploded, blood splashed upon all of them. That had caused Kenya to be pissed. Kenya at that point messed up.

Etain watched for a bit, but left when she was sure Catriona would win. She had Richard and James to deal with, and they would not kill themselves.

She did stop and help the rest of the group with some minions as the minions tried to drive them from the building. But the group prevented that, because going out into the public would put the normal people in danger. Put energy in danger. When she saw a group of minions, try to rush Timothy, she placed her hands on the ground and electrocuted the group. They fell dead. She just gave a nod and went to find Richard.

Etain went to find Richard trying to get into the vaults. "What are you doing, Richie?"

Richard turned, "you should show respect! I am OVERLORD! And I need the drugs in there for my next wife!"

Etain sneered at Richard. "You haven't been Overlord since you came and bowed to me. I should have killed you the moment you raped your wife. Oh, I know more than you think. Want to know the reason why I haven't? Your bride asked me not to kill you. She had been slowly poisoning you. She just needed to wait until the prenuptial term limits were over so she and her children gained it all."

"You are going against us for what? The ordinary people? These so-called friends of yours? Would you die for these beings, Arc? The Queen of Evil finally finds her heart?"

"I am willing to meet my maker. For them. I cannot save the world. I cannot have the world on my shoulders. But I can save my world. My brothers. My those I love. For my family, I am willing to meet my maker. Are you ready?"

"It won't be me meeting our maker, Arc."

"Oh, I doubt my maker is ready to meet me. But you, have a reservation in whatever damnation we are headed for when we leave this mortal world." With that, Etain let loose her power and surrounded Richard in a bubble of currents. "Say goodnight."

"Go to hell." Richard spat as his body started to convulse.

She moved over and used a dagger and cut off his penis, and stuffed it in his mouth. "Meet you there, rapist." With that Etain caused the current to go through his body and killed him. His body fell to the ground. She turned to Tony and Gabriel. "You two good?"

"Yes. Well done you." Tony helped Gabriel up. "Go on. We got the rest of these minions."

Etain nodded. There was James, but he should still be knocked out. So she wanted to go check on the others. She had seen William and Whalen fighting with Robert Evanson.

The rest of their group had been fighting the minions that would have attacked the moment Etain had made her announcement.

She had seen that Timothy and Moon were injured but would be fine. The minions were destroyed. She walked through dismembered bodies, heads, blood, but she had not lost anybody. But where was Catriona? Worry filled her, she waved her hand to Tony and Gabe and went looking for Catriona.

Etain was looking for Catriona. The battles have been hard fought. But it had been awhile since she had seen her partner. She was so concerned she did not notice James sneak up behind her and knock her

James was awakened by his assistant. He jumped up and grabbed the assistant by their neck and broke it. Absorbing the life force. He had to kill Etain. But, first, he had to break her. She was the ultimate challenge. And he would break her, then have her, and then he would kill her.

CHAPTER TWENTY-THREE
THE END

Catriona was looking for Etain. She went up to the top floor. She found a room of rubber. It would prevent Etain from shocking someone through the ground or walls. She gasped as saw Etain tied to the wall. She rushed over to try to get her down.

"So, she kept a hero hidden from us." A voice came up behind her, a sneer in his voice. "And such a pretty hero. Of course, Arc did always like pretty things. So, how long have you been her pet? What makes you so worthy to have been kept alive? Do you lay there and pleasure her? Maybe I will have a taste before I kill you in front of her."

Catriona moved to battle him, but he pushed a button and caused Etain to seize and throw a shock through the air, hitting her. as she was between Etain and this villain. "Who are you?" Villains liked to monologue, so get him talking, was a good plan. That way, she would have time to get through to Etain.

"I used to be a hero. You would have known me as The Warrior. But, there was no benefit in being a hero. So, I charged towns to save them. And eventually joined the winning side."

Catriona sneered, "a week man isn't going to win against us."

"Oh, but I think I have already. You see, this room also neutralizes the powers of all but one. And with me controlling Arc, you have no way to defeat me." James pressed the button again and Catriona fell to her knees. James walked over. "I am going to enjoy my time with you. After all, anything that Arc had picked for a pet has to be a good lay."

Catriona refused to scream as the electrical current flowed through her. "ARC! WAKE UP!" Catriona had to get through to Etain. Catriona had promised to help her. To carry her to the other side. That she would never be alone again. The words may not have all been said aloud, but the intentions were there. Other pretty words were exchanged. And Catriona wanted to know what it was like to tempt Etain.

What would it be like to love Etain, fully, with no restrictions or masks?

But Etain had to "WAKE UP!" She screamed the last as the thought went through her mind.

James brought out a knife and used it to slice at Catriona's outfit. She fought, but he hit her with a shock again. He chained her hands up to the wall. "Tsk, Tsk. You naughty girl you." He sliced her shirt in half. The leer on his face did not bode well for Catriona.

"ETAIN! HELP!" Catriona screamed, hoping it got through to her. That she would just wake up and fight. She knew Etain was strong. The strongest of both the former villains, the heroes of the old days, and for sure the strongest woman Catriona had ever met in her existence, even if Etain believed she was weak. Yes, she broke, but all it takes is one moment in time to make a persona the hero or the villain. And

Etain had nothing to make the scale tip to the hero side of things. She had lost all that.

Etain heard everything through a fog. She blinked as she heard to wake up. But what snapped her awake was Catriona yelling her name and help. Her eyes popped open, and she saw James wanting to rape her Catriona. She felt a fury she only had felt once before, when she was thirteen. She could not control her power, it flowed through her and had one goal. Kill James. She released it all. She threw it through the air, all directed towards him. It broke the chains that held her up. She floated over and kept shocking him. Letting the current flow through and burn his body. Etain knew of his motto, Long Live The Queen. "The Fake King is Dead. Long Live The Queen!" She sneered as she ran the currents through the now dead body.

Catriona stood, her own cuffs having been destroyed in the first blast. She blinked in shock at the power Etain held. She really could have killed her at any time. She blinked once more, James was dead. "Etain."

Etain turned, her eyes still wired, the electrical current still flowing around her body.

"Etain, he is dead. He didn't touch me like that. He is dead." Catriona had to bring her down. By this time other heroes had shown up, Tony in front. "Etain, he didn't touch me. I am fine."

"He didn't…"

"No. You stopped him. You saved me."

Etain dropped the electrical current, but her eyes were still wired. She moved over and grabbed Catriona's hand. "He didn't…"

"No. I am fine. I am fine. You saved me."

"Cat…" Etain finally let the energy drop and her eyes rolled back, and she fell into Catriona's arms.

Catriona caught her. She looked at the others. "Win?"

Tony smiled, "yeah, we won. Not bad for a bunch of retired heroes and a few villains, huh?"

"Wanna help me?" Catriona asked as she tried to hold up Etain.

Tony nodded and went over and scooped Etain up. "Let's get Arc home."

Once they got back to Etain's home and Catriona put Etain into her bed, she went back to the others. "Report?"

"All the villains of VilCorp fought to the death."

"Or we just plain killed them." Timothy stated. "What? I am a bad guy. The minions were good for a workout."

"Oh, please. You slipped. You are a firefighter in the town you settled in. You use your power of fire to put out fires." Tony rolled his eyes, "you gave up your bad guy ways."

"Bad guys have morals too. Killing innocents isn't any fun."

Tony laughed, "we did good for a bunch of has beens."

"Speak for yourself, Freedom. Pryo still gots it."

"Whatever, Tim. So, how long before she wakes up? We have got to party!"

"It is really just exhaustion, so probably tomorrow." At least, that is what Catriona hoped.

"Yes, well done you." Came a drawl. There stood Etain at the door.

"Should you be up?" Catriona went into a mother hen mode.

"I am fine. Exhausted, but fine. Nothing some sleep won't cure. The party can wait for tomorrow. I just wanted to make sure we all came out fine."

"Only minor injuries and all your former workers are dead." Tony stated, "I will cook dinner. Everybody rest! Tomorrow we party!"

Etain chuckled, "help me back to bed?"

Catriona nodded and wound an arm around her waist. "You really are okay, right?"

Etain smiled as she got into bed. "I am fine. Come, lay with me. I always dreamed of sleeping next to you."

Catriona nodded and went to change into some sleep pants and a tank top. "As long as you sleep. You need your rest."

"And I need to make sure you are here, and okay."

"I am more than okay. I am here with you. Sleep, foul fiend."

"Night, my sweet hero." Etain whispered as she let her exhaustion take her.

Catriona did not know how long she laid there just watching Etain breath, but soon she let her own exhaustion set in and take her to the land of nod.

The heroes and not so villain-ish villains were all sleeping off the battle when the news hit.

'BEINGS OF POWER AMONG US ONCE MORE!'

'MYTHS NO MORE! HEROES OF OLE LIVE'

'HEROES SAVE HUMANITY; BRINGS DOWN CORRUPTION'

'HEROES OF THE WORLD ALIVE ONCE MORE'

They would not know how much life was going to change in the morning. But that was a problem better left to the harsh light of dawn.

Etain dreamed of a world where she did not have to wear a mask. Where when people looked at her in the clear light of dawn they would see who she was and not run. No longer hiding in the light of the setting sun and the mask she created. If they did not accept her, at least Catriona accepted her. Catriona looked at her over the cold and pure morning dew, seeing the damaged soul beneath her act. With Catriona and her friends, she no longer was afraid to show the world who she was, the good and the bad. The world may still be blinded by the heat of the setting sun, and see only parts of her that make up her mask. But Catriona caught the small flicker of light in her soul that was surrounded by darkness that was darker than the purest black. For the flicker of light tells the truth; her soul was not as black as coal that she wanted the world to assume. No. She built a mask of evil to protect the only pure thing left in her soul, the flicker of light that told her right from wrong. That had her killing to save a child. Had her risking everything, including her life, to save humanity. And in her sleep, she dreamed of a world where that mask could forever be removed from her shoulders.

CHAPTER TWENTY-FOUR
HAPPILY EVER AFTER?

Etain knew she was lucky. To be with Catriona. Her life seemed to be perfect now. It took losing almost everything she thought she wanted to get to this point. Maybe the Norns were not useless beings after all. Etain still enjoyed the finer things, wines perfectly aged, whiskeys older that most mortals, expensive shoes, clothes, and homes. She lost count of the tattoos she had that painted her life from birth to now. She fell in love again, with someone funnier and smarter than herself. And most of all, due to this person, she finally believed she could be happy, at peace, and most of all safe without being feared. Her Catriona was like the knight that came to battle the dragon to save the princess, only to discover the dragon was the Queen, and loved her despite her fire breathing ways. Thus, saving the Queen and gaining her heart.

Etain smiled as she thought of that. Catriona had her heart as no other had it before. Oh, her first loves had a place in her heart. All first loves did. But Catriona seen her at her worst, and now Etain just wanted to give Catriona, her sweet hero, her best. This year had changed her. A year ago, she was watching her world collapse. Now she had a love of her existence at her side. She had friends. Real friends. Not those who wanted something from her, so tolerated her. Tony and Gabriel seemed to have snuck their way into her heart, too. They were close as siblings.

And she was sure something was going on between them. Her trickster brothers. She hummed. Yes, life was finally back on track.

And best of all, Christmas was coming.

Etain may celebrate Yule, but Catriona loved Christmas.

And they were going to dinner tonight.

And on this lovely cold December day, and Catriona being back i Europe for the first time in centuries, Etain was going to ask, yes, ask and not just tell, Catriona to actually be hers for eternity.

Catriona looked over at Etain. Once upon a time, in her darke thoughts, she thought of what it would be like to give in to Etain How it would balance them and the greatest fight between them was would take out the trash. And finally, it did not have to be a da thought. It became the shining light of a saving grace!

She was with Etain.

Not Arc.

But Etain.

And it was great.

It had been a year since the battle that destroyed VilCor During that year, Etain had started a new business. Restoring, copying, and translating ancient documents, she had named it Catriona. Not shocking. Her sister is what set her upon her p this life, though she lost her way. And Catriona was the one put her back on the path Etain had wanted out of this life.

Etain specialized in languages. Having been around for thousand years, and having an eidetic memory, she soaked up languages as she traveled the world. She actually loved languages. And when she was translating, nothing got 'lost' in translations. In fact, Etain had made it her goal to retranslate lots of 'holy' and religious texts. Let's just say, Etain may have come over to the side of the angels, but she will never, ever, be an angel.

Except to one person.

The person she called many things, sweetheart, darling, dearest, and Catriona's favorite, sweet hero. Etain even using different languages when introducing Catriona when they were out. Kjaereste, meaning the dearest, being the most popular, but every so often, when Etain was mad at Catriona, she would be introduced as mulkvisti, which translated roughly to the one not hated as much as others. Catriona had noticed she hated the words girlfriend and partner. Lover was okay. So, Catriona just introduced Etain as her fallen angel. For honestly, Catriona thought, that is exactly how to best explain Etain.

Etain had fallen into darkness because of love turned grief. But Etain was still an angel. Just one that understood both the light and the dark, and thus of Earth. Not of good. Not of evil. Just perfectly human, and thus of both.

Catriona smiled as Etain gathered her papers. They were in London for an auction. There was a set of scrolls from 2500 BCE China that Etain wanted to win. Catriona had left the bakery in the hands of Gabriel and Tony. Maybe not the best thing to do, but since they had become Etain's best friends and something or other themselves, they had stuck around the middle of nowhere in Iowa to be close to family.

Family.

Catriona thought she lost the chance for that a long time ago.

But she had learned blood does not make family.

Family was who supported with all their souls.

Family was who fought side by side.

Bonds of loyalty and choice are the strongest forged.

The blood of the covenant is thicker than the water of the womb.

That is true.

Those who stand by you, who have been in battle at your side, they are family.

Like one of Etain's favorite shows said: Family does not end in blood.

And it for sure did not have to start there either.

Because through everything, in the end, family just does not end.

Etain was smirking as she walked out of the auction. She got everything she wanted, and then some just to mess with people. Catriona sighed as they left. But if this was the most evil thing Etain did these days, she would deal with it.

"So, how about dinner?" Catriona asked as she grabbed Etain's hand.

"You can choose, my hero." Etain hummed as they walked down the street hand in hand, content in having destroyed some people's evening.

Catriona got Etain to the Ritz, they were going to have dinner at the Ritz, something Catriona always wanted to do, and now she was here with the right person. She and Etain had been dating for six months.

Not before that, as Etain went through her early days of therapy, and it had brought a lot of nightmares back to the surface and there had been fights and screaming. Also, William stated for Etain's mental health she should not date before she made a certain break through. But Catriona had refused to let her leave and give up. But Etain had worked through things, and had torn down the walls around the light in her soul, brick by brick.

"This is awful fancy for you, Cat." Etain stated as she picked up a wine list. Etain learned Catriona did not like fancy. Where Etain hid in fancy trappings.

"Always wanted to dine at the Ritz."

"Well, even I never dined here. This is a place for a couple. In my opinion."

"Well, here we are. Etain…" Catriona bit her lip.

"Not that you biting your lip doesn't make a pretty picture and cause a whole lot of naughty images in my head. What has you nervous, my sweet hero?"

"I know we are not normal people."

"Normal is an illusion, sold to the public to prevent individuals from being themselves."

"I am trying to say something here, you foul fiend."

"Okay, sorry, go on my dear, and I won't interrupt again."

"Good." Catriona took a breath. She listened to the song that started playing, she snorted, A Nightengale Sang in Berkley Square, Etain was obsessed with that song. "So, we are not normal, but I was wondering, if," Catriona got down on a knee and opened a ring box. "You would be mine for eternity, Marry me my heart?"

Etain stared at the simple Claddagh ring with a chocolate diamond heart. She looked up into Catriona's eyes. "Yes." She pulled her up and kissed her deeply, ignoring the clapping in the room.

Catriona blushed and pulled back, putting the ring on Etain. "I love you."

Etain pulled a ring from her pocket. It too was a Claddagh ring, but instead it had a blue diamond. She took her hand. "I love you. I was going to ask after we left. You are mine, for eternity." And she pulled Catriona back to her to kiss her. "Mine." Etain whispered against Catriona's lips. After all, Etain was still extremely possessive of what was hers.

Perhaps, even a villain could have a Happily Ever After.

VILCORP

About the Author

Meet Kris Charles.
Creator and Destroyer of Worlds.

Kris Charles is a pen name. They live in Iowa. They enjoys music, baking, and playing with a Pup named Milo Roy.

Katy Lily was their first major story, starting in 1992, it was told as a verbal story to their youngest brother. Parts were used as short stories for classes from grade school to College. And now, all ten year of Katherine Lillian's Life will be published for the world to read.

Kris is also the author of A Guardian's Life Saga; first novel is The Seven Deadlies. The author of The Keepers Trilogy; first novel is The Keepers and the Sisters of Lilith. Others coming soon include Darkened Grace, The Demon Within, and Praying.

www.ingramcontent.com/pod-product-compliance
Lightning Source LLC
Chambersburg PA
CBHW070559180626
46817CB00005B/1906